Metaphorosis

January 2018

Beautifully made speculative fiction

Metaphorosis

January 2018

edited by
B. Morris Allen

Metaphorosis Books

Neskowin

ISSN: 2573-136X (online)
ISBN: 978-1-64076-100-1 (e-book)
ISBN: 978-1-64076-103-2 (paperback)

January 2018

The Seer at Sunset Hills Shopping Plaza

Katherine Perdue

"A woman's been murdered!"

That was Theodora Yates for you: always jumping to conclusions, bless her heart, and that conclusion most often of all. But there was no talking her out of it once she'd made up her mind, so I said, without bothering to ask any questions, "Then we must go to the Seer at once!"

My granddaughter, Katie, she didn't think much of us going to the Seer. She grew up in this new world: it was no more magical or difficult for her than breathing air. Once, she asked me, "Granny, how much did you just pay that woman for something they'd give you for free at the library? Or you could do it yourself. I'll teach you how to Google if you want." She waved a tiny glowing screen in front of my face.

"You can't Boolean with Google," I said, deeply offended.

"Granny!" She stretched out the word so that I would understand her exasperation. "You don't even know what that means!"

"No, I don't. But it's what the Seer says, and I trust her."

Katie wasn't exactly wrong about the library. Theodora and I used to go round there every time she got it in her head that someone had been murdered, but there were a great many things that the librarians believed were none of our business. And what about the police, you might wonder? Well, they were worse than the librarians. They always just called Katie to come get us and take us home. We never had problems like that with the Seer.

It was a hike to get there. The Seer worked out of a strip mall just off the highway on the edge of town, and I didn't drive anymore because of my cataracts. We looked into getting one of those new-fangled automated cars, but it turned out you still needed a license to operate one of them, though I couldn't guess why. The doctor took my license away years ago. Theodora's doctor told her she shouldn't drive; the exact reason escaped her. She still had her license though. Her doctor was nicer than mine and took pity when she said she needed it for emergencies, since she didn't have any family.

Going to the Seer about a murder never qualified as an emergency, so we took the bus halfway and then we walked, even though there was no sidewalk. A couple of cars honked at us, but I shook my cane at them and they kept on going.

Theodora told me about the murder on the way. It seemed a car had been left parked in her driveway overnight.

"The same one as last week?" I interrupted. Theodora lived near campus. Students were always leaving their cars anywhere they could fit them and you know the sort of hours students keep. About noon or one o'clock, they would stagger back and drive off, unless the car had been towed. You wouldn't believe how persecuted they proclaimed themselves to be if the owner of the driveway had the effrontery to tow their car!

But Theodora never called the tow truck. She always assumed that the owner of the car had been murdered.

"Last week? Was there one last week? No, I don't think it's the same."

"Don't you think it's just another student?"

"No, I do not," said Theodora with a particularly forceful thrust of her cane. I had offended her and she wouldn't say another word to me till we got to the Seer's.

Strip malls are always dreary, but Sunset Hills Shopping Plaza took the cake. The empty husk of a now defunct supermarket dominated the row. "Closed for Renovation," the sign said. I knew that's what it said because I read it back when it was new. All you could tell now is that one of the letters printed on it might have been an 'R'.

Next to it was Video World; vacant, of course. Then a vending machine selling camera film. We'd seen the truck come by to restock it. Sunset Hills was the kind of place that drew lost things like that. Lost people too. There was always a huddle of them in the mornings and the evenings near the old supermarket, waiting eagerly to press around the occasional pickup truck that stopped there to take aboard a lucky few. Migrants, I assumed. People who'd left their homes behind but never quite found one here.

At the end of the row there was a Chinese restaurant that was still in business, although I'd never seen anyone go in it. And across from that was the Seer.

We didn't know her name. She said she didn't tell anybody. Knowing a person's true name gave you power over that person. No one had power over the Seer.

She had a wooden sign that swung back and forth eerily and creaked a bit — when the wind was right. It was purple with a moon and some stars rising above a crystal ball with an open palm beneath it. And, decorated with gold-trimmed purple cloth: a computer monitor. She had all that in neon on her window too, and the words: Psychic, Palm Reading, Digital Second Sight, Computer Repair. The Seer did a bit of everything.

We went in the plate glass door and through a beaded curtain into a room where the air was thick with incense and the walls were all lined with dark curtains. Mystical symbols were painted on the ceiling and there was a black-light to make them glow. We headed for the back room, which was an ordinary office with a desk and a computer, an antique flat-screen with an ancient keyboard dating back from the time when people thought all computer equipment had to be grey. There was a couch for clients and a straight-backed chair that the Seer put in just for Theodora because she couldn't sit on a couch with her back the way it was. The Seer knew we didn't need any of that nonsense in the front room. When we came, it was for real magic.

She stood up as we came in. "I foresaw your coming and made tea," she said solemnly and went to pour it for us. She had a security camera set up in the parking lot, so she did a lot of very localized foreseeing. I think she knew Theodora and I knew, but we never said anything about it. We didn't want to take away her fun. And we liked having the tea ready. "I take it there has been another murder?"

"Yes," I said. "Terrible affair. Theodora, tell her about it."

"Well," said Theodora, with a bit of a quaver in her voice. "I don't know that there's so much to tell. There was a car left in my driveway last night. It's still there."

"She says it isn't the same one as last week," I added.

Theodora gave me a glare. "Don't be spiteful, Nancy. It's different this time. When I found it, the door was open. And someone had knocked out the window. It's a stolen car, I'm sure of it. And someone just left it in my driveway."

"It just sounds to me like someone broke in while it was in your driveway," I said. "Nothing you've said makes it sound stolen."

Theodora crossed her arms and said nothing, turning a long-suffering gaze in appeal to our host.

The Seer ran a hand over the small crystal ball she kept on her desk. "If someone had broken the window in the driveway, there would have been glass all over the seat. And there was no glass, was there?" Theodora smirked. "Do you have the license plate for me?"

"And the VIN. I know you like to have the true names of things." She passed a slip of paper to the Seer.

"Very good." The Seer laid her hands down reverently upon the keyboard, whereupon it began to glow softly, while at the same time the lights in the room dimmed and just a touch of fog began to drift across the desk.

"Nice," I commented. The Seer just smiled and started typing.

"It *is* a stolen car," she said after a moment. "Belongs to a Mr. James P. Garst. Not from around here. He reported it missing yesterday."

"That doesn't make any sense," Theodora muttered.

The Seer held out her hand and looked at Theodora. Theodora gave her the driver's license she had found on the front seat. "It's what made me think there must be something really wrong. You wouldn't just leave your license like that unless there were something wrong."

"'Hailey Grace Garst,'" the Seer read off the card. "Well, let's see what we can find out about Hailey Grace." Again she stretched out her hands and the keyboard lit. A few keystrokes later, she frowned. "She's been cursed."

"Cursed?" Theodora and I chorused. We'd heard of curses—who hadn't?—but usually they fell upon especially sanctimonious politicians or corporations that had angered the more anarchist factions of the web. This was the first we'd seen one used against an ordinary private citizen.

"Yes," said the Seer, turning the screen so that we could see. "You're looking at the Shallows right now. What anybody would see if they ran a search on Hailey Grace Garst. The first result:" she clicked and we saw it. Medical records. "If this is to be believed, Hailey Grace was committed to Spring Creek Psychiatric Hospital when she was fifteen for severe depression and suicidal ideation." She scrolled. "Released when she was sixteen. The doctors gave her a good report. Prescribed antidepressants. Pronounced her cured."

The Seer hit the back button. "And this is the second result." She clicked.

"Dearie me," said Theodora.

The photographs had been labeled helpfully in big, bold, red print with an arrow and the caption: "NOT HER HUSBAND!!!"

"That could explain the curse," I said.

The Seer clicked back again and showed us the rest of the results. Page after page of forum posts titled things like: "DO NOT HIRE THIS WOMAN!!!" and "DO NOT TRUST MENTAL PATIENT WITH UR KIDS".

"Well, maybe they shouldn't," I said. Theodora gave me a look.

"That is what a reasonable person might conclude if her access were limited to the Shallows," said the Seer. I believe it was meant as a gentle reproof to the both of us, but Theodora puffed up with vindication.

"But we're not confined to the Shallows!" added the Seer with enthusiasm. She waved her hands a bit theatrically and the air seemed almost to shimmer for a moment, as though the universe had just blinked. I'm not sure how she did it. "Behold!"

On the screen in the corner, there was a clock, and as she spoke, it began to tick backwards. "If we had looked yesterday, this is what we would have seen." The page was the same. The clock spun faster. "A week ago. A month ago. Six." And then, in a stage whisper, "Before the curse."

The clock stopped. The Seer clicked. We watched a video of a bride and groom waltzing under a banner that read, "Welcome to the wedding scrapbook of Hailey Grace Lowell Garst and James Prichard Garst. Congratulations Hailey and Jim!" The video was dated five years ago.

"She stole the car from her husband, then?" I asked.

Theodora was shaking her head. "She was carjacked in her husband's car and then murdered!"

The Seer smiled her patient smile and said nothing.

The next result was the divorce case. It had been ugly. But there was no mention of infidelity. The Seer checked the dates on the incriminating photographs. "Taken after the divorce," she said. "The man in the pictures may not have been her husband, but at the time, no man was."

"What about the medical records?" I asked. "Were they real?"

The Seer nodded. She was still looking at the court page. "It seems that after the divorce, Hailey Grace sued James Garst for defamation and for publishing private health records. But they couldn't prove anything because whoever laid the curse did it from a public computer. And it turns out that Spring Creek Psychiatric Hospital accidentally published all of its patients' records online three years ago. They've since apologized and taken them down, but who knows who could have copied them while they were up."

"Did she sue the hospital too?"

"There's a class-action going on. I would guess that in ten years or so she might get ten bucks off that. In the meantime..."

She showed us a page from the Springfield Herald Tribune. The headline read, 'Parents Raise Outcry Over Kindergarten Teacher's Mental Health'.

"She resigned a week later."

"Because of the curse," I said.

"Because of the curse."

"What about the baby?" Theodora asked, out of the blue, like she always did.

The Seer and I demanded together, "What baby?"

Theodora apologetically drew a few photographs out of her purse. Polaroids as usual. She had a huge stockpile of film cartridges in her basement and I suppose if she ever ran out, there was that vending machine. She gave each one a good shake before laying it down on the desk for us to see, though the image was already as clear as it would ever be.

First: the car in the driveway, the rear passenger-side door hanging open and the driver's window empty of glass.

Next: the license lying abandoned on the seat. The keys were still in the ignition.

And last, Theodora held it back a moment and when she finally laid it on the desk, her hand hesitated before pulling back to let us see: a baby seat strapped in the back on the passenger's side, next to the open door.

The Seer and I stared at it a moment and then she turned back to the screen. The keys clattered, the mouse wheel clicked. "She lost custody," the Seer said in a flat voice. "She'd lost her job and was struggling to pay rent on her apartment. Every new job she applied to, they ran a search on her and the curse took them in its thrall. She never even got an interview. And she couldn't move to a cheaper apartment because landlords wouldn't rent to her unless she had a job. She presented all this in court and the judge was sympathetic, but she said it wasn't a healthy environment for a child."

She turned the screen towards us again. On it was a picture of Hailey Grace holding her infant son. She wore a long green dress, cut a bit like a robe. Long dark hair in braids fell down her back. She was gaunt and beautiful in a Pre-Raphaelite way; it made her seem frail. But the way she looked at her son, the joy and the pride, the possessive way she held

19

him, it devoted me to her cause that instant.

"So it was a kidnapping," Theodora said slowly, "not a murder at all. What are we going to do?"

"Notify the police," said the Seer, at exactly the same time that I said, "We can't tell the police." We frowned at each other. Usually if anyone wanted to go to the police, it was me. Usually Theodora's murders turned out to be nothing and no one said anything at all about going to the police.

"What do you think?" I asked Theodora. She'd be on my side, of course. Nobody on earth had a softer heart than Theodora.

But I was wrong. "I suppose it is a crime," she said slowly.

"You would take a child away from his own mother?" I demanded. "I know you never had any children yourself, but I thought you'd at least understand —"

"I understand being alone," she said. And she did. She'd never married. She used to teach English at the university and she'd told me then that she didn't need children; she had students. But students weren't the same. She realized that after she retired. "I don't want to take a child away from his mother. Nor do I want to take him away from his father, his grandparents, his aunts and uncles, his whole life. That's what we're really talking about here, Nancy."

I said nothing. There was nothing to argue with in what she'd said.

"We don't know that James Garst isn't a wonderful father," she continued.

"But he cursed her!" I said.

"We don't know that. If we did — Can you find out?" she asked the Seer. "Was James Garst really the one who laid the curse?"

"Maybe." The Seer pursed her lips and turned back to the computer. There were no special effects this time. She typed and scrolled and glowered at the monitor and typed some more, the rhythm of tapped keys as steady and soothing as rain. Theodora and I waited and sipped our tea. Then she let out a quiet "a-ha."

"It was him," she said. "He signed on to his email while he was doing it. One of the forums he posted on followed his cookie crumbs back to his email and sold the information to advertisers. And to me."

"Then we can't go to the police," said Theodora. "It's black magic, cursing people. James Garst took that woman's whole future from her. He poisoned her very identity. You wouldn't give a child back to someone like that."

"No," said the Seer, "I wouldn't. But I am not a judge and don't want to be one."

"You are though," I said. "There's no middle ground in this. Can't cut the baby in half. Call the police, Hailey Grace goes to jail, and you've chosen the father's side. Don't call, and you've chosen the mother's."

The Seer looked unhappy.

"Lift the curse," said Theodora. "You can, can't you? No, better than that, can you make her invisible? Maybe post an obituary?"

"I'm not sure that's not black magic." The Seer looked again at the screen. It was back to the picture of mother and child. "I could make it as though she never existed. Delete every reference to her everywhere; all the court documents, credit reports, student loans, everything. Every record of that car ever existing too."

"A fresh start," I said.

"No start at all. Maybe when you were both young, it was possible to move to a new place with a new name and reinvent yourself, no documentation required. Not anymore. She couldn't get by just being *no one.* She'd need to find a person like me to make her into *someone*, and people like me charge a lot of money for a thing as precious as a new name and new life to go with it. We don't do it for charity and we don't always have a person's best interest at heart."

"You would do it for charity," I persisted.

The Seer laughed. "I would do it for my usual fee. But the thing is, I can't. Erasing her is powerful magic. Dangerous. Criminal, of course, though that's no concern of mine. Still, it's simple and I could do it in a day. But building her back up is something else: alchemy. It takes time and affinity. I cannot do it from a distance. I cannot do it without her consent and cooperation."

Theodora and I didn't see the problem. "So we find her and bring her to you," I said. "It shouldn't be hard. This isn't a big place and she doesn't have a car. She must be nearby." We dismissed the objection that she could have gotten on a bus. They checked IDs on buses nowadays. The Seer was right. Having no identity was worse than having a cursed one.

She rested her chin upon her fist and sat for a while in thought. "You really think you can find her?"

"Yes," I said, and then, sensing that she was wavering and pressing my advantage, I went too far. "You said it yourself. We pay your fee, and this is what we're asking you to do."

There was a long silence. I held my breath. Finally she said, "The customer is always right, or so I've been told. I'll do it. It'll take me all night. In the meantime, you'd better get rid of that car."

We drove it into the lake. Well, Theodora drove it, since she had her license. I told her that it was silly to care about licenses when you were driving a stolen car into the lake, but she held firm. And the next day we went back to the Seer's and she showed us: Hailey Grace Lowell Garst had been erased. Searching for her in the Shallows brought up nothing at all. The divorce case was gone. When we put in the case number, an entirely different case came up.

"Won't they have backups?" I asked.

"I have my ways of getting to them as well," said the Seer.

"And when James Garst goes to the police station to report his son missing?"

She smiled. "They won't be able to help him. They'll find no record in any database that he ever had a son. When he gives them social security numbers for the boy and Hailey Grace, they'll come up invalid. The only records are on paper, and no one cares about paper anymore. It isn't real if it isn't digital."

All the next week I kept expecting the police to show up on our doorsteps looking for Hailey Grace. Nothing happened. Nor, for all that we turned over every stone and branch, did we find any sign of our missing mother and child. Whenever I thought of them, I worried that we had not done them a kindness in the end.

We didn't go back to the Seer's for some time after that. We were embarrassed that we hadn't lived up to our end of the bargain and for me, it was more than that. I was worried we'd make it to Sunset Hills and find the Seer's shop just as empty as Video World. That was the way of places like hers, appearing suddenly out of nothing and gone again without warning or trace. I'd crossed a line with her by insisting, and I wasn't sure she'd forgive it.

But days went by, then a month, and inevitably Theodora had new mysteries to investigate. I could only put her off for so long. So we made the long trek back to the strip mall and I'd never been so glad in my life to see purple velvet and lit neon.

As we were crossing the parking lot, I saw a waitress taking her break outside the Chinese restaurant. She was thin and had long dark hair. She looked familiar. I only caught a glimpse of her before she went back inside, but the Seer looked awfully jolly about something she'd seen on her security camera when we came in.

"How'd you find her?" I asked, expecting some grand feat of magic, something far beyond my abilities. But the answer was simpler than that.

"I looked out my window," said the Seer, "and there she was, standing in the parking lot with all the others looking for work. I waited till she was one of the only ones left; she doesn't have the right build for hard labor. Then I went out and asked if she'd ever done any waitressing. Xiaomi is a friend of mine and I knew she had an opening."

She hesitated a moment, looking a little unsure of her ground. Up until that point, our relationship had always been strictly business. "Either of you care to get lunch after we're done here? The Chinese place is actually pretty good and I'd like to introduce you to Hailey. It's traditional for fairy godmothers to come in threes."

About the story

The idea for this story came to me while working at the library reference desk. An undergraduate asked me a simple question. I looked up the answer. The student thanked me a thousand times and was in awe as though I'd performed some sophisticated magic. I thought about it for a while and realized, it's not that different from magic. It follows the same rules. If you know the true name of something—the correct subject heading for library materials, a good keyword for a search engine—that's all you need to summon it forth.

I was also doing a lot of programming at the time and there the connection is even clearer. With words alone, with code, you can compose a spell that has some physical effect on the world, whether that's changing the color of pixels on a screen or animating a robot.

We all use this kind of "magic" day in and day out. We don't notice the miracles in front of us. I wanted to tell a story about characters who do notice them and who afford them the same awe as that undergraduate at the reference desk.

A question for the author

Q: Do you use music for inspiration? If so what do you listen to?

A: Yes. Sometimes this is straightforward. If I'm trying to write something sad, I don't choose upbeat music. If it's difficult to write, then I avoid distractingly catchy lyrics. But I also find that if I've written productively while listening to something before, especially if more than once, that piece of music gets imbued with the moment, becomes a kind of talisman. So that if I want to write that way again, with that kind of focus, I have but to listen to it. As for what kind? You name it: opera, bluegrass, rock, gamelan, all kinds.

About the author

Katherine Perdue lives in Virginia with her two cats and many fish and works as a librarian at a small university. She loves linguistics, live music, and tropical plants.

Jewel/Gem Offering

Emily McIntyre

It is dawn in the half-world of Varuzza,
and the sun strikes the woman's face in
strips of meat red and blue. Around her
still-trim waist she wears a leather belt
holstering the latest shiny aggro-tech; old
lace kisses pearls around her neck and in
her hand is a pot holding the tender sprig
of a rose with deep purple thorns and a
bud the color of midnight on the old Home
World. Two days ago, she left the
technological nightmare of Greatcity
behind and turned the nose of her
hovercraft north, toward a backwater of
the universe. The rose fills the cab with a
young, piney poison but she no longer

notices;   until   the   moment   she
relinquishes it she is impervious.

Years   as   a   high-paid   whore   in   the
faraway Wilder West world taught her to
seize her joy where she found it; a lifetime
of governmental intrigue confirmed joy is
an illusion. Still, she feels a choke of
emotion when she sees the curving dome
of her daughter's holdfast clinging to
blasted earth with the same kind of
tenacity with which she herself has clung
to vestiges of freedom gathered through
the years in dribs and drabs of pilfered
data.

Like   any   stranger,   she   waits   in   a
generic room after the vac-lock. Remnants
of her beauty veil her still, but they are
drawn taut, like the pale skin on her
cheekbones. Waiting, hardly a breath stirs
her. Seven years of searching and a
lifetime   of   regret   culminate   in   this
moment, in the hiss of the door as a small
woman enters with a line of half-hostile
puzzlement creasing between her winglike
brows   and   a   dowdy   turquoise   tunic
straining over her belly. The traveler
stands   and   extends   the   rose   sprig;
automatically the other woman takes it
and the fingers of her right hand close
against its stem; the left cup its pot. The

single black bud glows against the synthetic fabric covering her breasts. The two women stand like that for long breaths, waiting for a script that does not exist. Finally, the traveler says, "You know who I am." It sounds like a statement, but her voice carries bald hope.

In answer there is only silence. The rose between them is a banner of failure. Infinite potential ignored for too long; the rose-magic heritage that should be passed in whispers and rituals between the generations instead handed over like a reluctant hostage at the end. The daughter looks down at the rose. Her hair is parted in a meandering line and has not been washed recently. The long pause causes the older woman to stir on her feet, to cock her head so that one dangling russet jewel brushes her shoulder.

"I learned you married an itinerant," she says, her prejudice coloring her voice and bringing an angry flush to the other woman's cheek. An itinerant, scum, a meandering prophet with nothing to his name but this desolate holding far away from everything that matters, on the harshest inhabited planet in the multiverse.

The younger woman's eyes narrow along her fine cheekbones—familiar cheekbones. The rose twitches with her tightened grasp, sends eddies of its rich perfume through the room. "Why do you care?" The perfume makes the traveler dizzy, now that she is not the rose's mistress and is susceptible to its power. She struggles to find coherence. Fear chokes her more surely than any over-zealous client ever has.

I care, she thinks to say, because my daughter deserves better. I care, she almost answers, because he will leave you broken and alone and you will regret your life like I regret mine. You can never count on men. But she says only, "Because I cannot help it." She lost the right to care the same day she delivered a mewling girl to the harsh world in a rush of blood and forgetfulness. The day she rose from her bed and disappeared to start her life over on another planet—the day she broke the chain of magic that extended hundreds of years back through the women of her line. She can feel the bitterness twisting her once-famed lips.

At least let her leave well. She steps toward her daughter. "You know what the rose is?" She almost thinks the rose listens, that its poisonous thorns tremble a little at the thought of leaving her. That the Jewel/Gem yearns for its former caretaker; but that is foolish. Magical/chemical or not, a rose is just a plant, not a friend. Not a friend, just a poison so subtle it is imbued with the very desires of its keeper and so old it is undetectable by all modern poison-sniffers.

Her daughter opens her mouth to answer and thinks better of it. She swallows her words, tucks her nail-bitten fingers together around the slick belly of the flower pot. It is clear she knows exactly what she holds; maybe her blood sparks with recognition the way the traveler's did the day her mother died and left her holding the pot. Maybe she has heard the rumors; when you hold the plant the Emperor would trade his planet for, you don't need to say much. When you hold a magic so potent a single drop can change history, you can straighten your back a little. You have, you might think, a way out. A second chance. A fallback.

A child cries, closer now. The younger woman shivers as if waking from a dream, but before she can turn to leave, the traveler reaches out one hand and traces the sweet curve of her daughter's cheek for the second time in her life. The cheek is not so soft as it was in the moment of birth and forgetting, but it is still softer than anything the traveler has felt before. As her hand falls it catches, too familiar, on the spiky edges of Jewel/Gem and she leaves a pendant drop of blood there, cradled against one of the dark thorns which have never pricked her before. Perhaps it was intentional. Once she held her daughter's fate in her hands; now the roles are reversed.

Even after she leaves, she feels the softness lingering on her fingers for hours, like the familiar scent of Jewel/Gem poison now growing and filling her lungs. Her breathing grows thick—the tendons stand out on her long neck with the effort of it. This is, it seems, her daughter's wish; Jewel/Gem is merely an extension of its caretaker's will. She accepts the knowledge and the poison. It is her time.

She is a legend on six planets within her lifetime. All forgotten now; forgotten except the softness of her daughter's cheek on the tips of her fingers. Joy is hard to recognize—she's had so little practice—but perhaps it is joy that fills her when she points her hovercraft into oblivion and lowers the sunshield. Perhaps it is joy she feels in the sacred moment before her skin chars and the pearls melt into her neck. That, or a commonplace kind of redemption.

About the story

Summer in Portland is a riot of roses. Funereal roses, scattering their fragile petals around them like Miss Havisham's train; glowing roses like tiny sun-bits just waiting to be noticed; classic tea roses whispering of the past. I spend a lot of time on my bike in the summer in this city, thinking while I ride, and occasionally I pull over and lose myself in one of the many rose parks in the city. I set my helmet to the side and lie on my back so the sun and filter through the serrated leaves to kiss my cheeks.

Summer 2017 I had about three weeks when everything seemed a rose-scented dream. I remembered the family legend of my great-great-great grandmother's pink rose, which she brought down the Ohio river with her, and which nearly every female family member has grown from a little slip in a Mason jar of water. (I've killed two in my many cross-country moves.) I began to think about the way the things we inherit from our families are rarely the things we want, but sometimes the things we need. I thought about my own writer-mother, and my storytelling daughter. I wondered what would happen if roses were magical, and only women could wield them? And then I thought of the strange way desire and betrayal seem wound into every interaction we have with our parents, our children, and that was the beginning of "Jewel/Gem Offering".

I still envision exploring the concept more thoroughly. A book would be a better idea, but I love flash fiction and all it hides and reveals. This was my first sci-fi story and I had to laugh when I realized it still had magic in it. I guess I'm an inveterate magic-seeker, wherever my imagination takes me.

A question for the author

Q: Why fantasy?

A: Ignoring the fact that Jewel/Gem is a sci-fi story (my first, possibly my last), I choose to write fantasy not just because it's cool—like fezzes are cool—but because life, through the lens of fantasy, is a little richer. Through fantasy I can take a stab at the 'why' behind the 'how', and often neglect the 'how' entirely. In fantasy we can tackle tough topics with just enough distance to stay safe until the fatal moment that truth stabs us in the heart and we find that, like all good literature, this story has changed us somehow. We're bigger. Deeper. Angrier.

Fantasy helps us live.

About the author

A globe-trotting coffee entrepreneur by day and a diehard fantasy writer/reader by night, Emily McIntyre lives in Portland, Oregon.

@mcintyrewrites

This Side of the Wall

Michael Gardner

Today was my day to choose a disease.

"Fennel," Mama called up from the kitchen. "Breakfast's near ready."

"Coming, Mama," I yelled back as I pulled a simple, blue dress over my head. I tied my hair back tight, laced up my shoes and then ran down the stairs to the kitchen.

Mama was heavily pregnant again. She was stirring a large pot that bubbled away on the stove, filling the air with the aroma of milk and oats. Sage, Lentil, and Chilli were crawling around Mama's ankles, squealing. Strawberry, Colander, Rosemary, and Tommy sat at the table, spoons in hands, waiting for their porridge.

Mama had the birthing disease. "When you have the birthing disease," Mama would say, "you don't have time to dilly dally picking out the perfect name for your little uns. I like to look at what's nearby when the baby comes and pick a name that way." Mama had been cooking just before I was born on the kitchen floor. Mama had been cooking before most of our births.

Pa sat at the head of the table, stiff backed. His raw, cracked hands rested in bowls of ice and his stone-grey eyes watched the children. I gave his hard shoulder a squeeze as I walked past him and made my way to the opposite end of the table.

Pa had laid-to-waste disease. He worked in demolition, destroying buildings with his rock-hard hands. When he was young, those hands had been harder than diamonds. But not anymore. As he grew older, it was like the hardness in his hands had begun to leak from where he needed it and, instead, it was spreading slowly but surely up his arms and across his chest and face. The money was too good to stop working, so Pa persisted, despite the toll on his body, despite the stiffness in his joints and the limited movement. I guess it made me sad, though Mama said it shouldn't. We all have to bear our diseases, the good and the bad.

Pa directed his grey gaze at me and cleared his throat. He didn't speak much normally — the hardness in his jaw made talking difficult. But he would speak today, I knew. He would give me the same speech he had given to my older brothers and sisters. The one he reserved for all of our sixteenth name days.

His jaw cracked loudly as he forced his mouth open. His lips were brittle and dry and hard flakes of grey skin fell as he spoke.

"Happy ... name day ... Fennel," he forced out. "I don't know ... how much longer ... I can earn ... for the family," he rasped. I craned forward to listen. "So now ... it's time for you ... to give back." A dry red tongue darted out and flicked at his lips, but it barely wet the surface. "Take this money ... and invest it ... in a disease ... that will allow you ... to earn for the family." He removed a wet hand from the ice and reached into his pocket. He withdrew five one hundred dollar notes and pushed them roughly towards the middle of the table. "Invest it wisely, Fennel ... like your brothers ... like your sisters." He dipped his hand back into the ice, grimacing as the cold bit into his wounds.

I reached for the money on the table. More money than I had ever seen. Enough to buy any disease I wanted.

"What are you going to contract, Fennel?" Rosemary asked as she stared at her reflection in her spoon.

"Yeah, Fennel. What are you gonna get?" chimed in Tommy. "A taking disease like Knife?"

My brother Knife was only a year older than me. We'd always been close, even sharing a room up until he'd contracted the taking disease and moved out on his own. Now, people paid him to bear diseases they had contracted that just didn't work out like they thought they should. He'd done well for the family, but I couldn't see him lasting more than another year or two. It was a wealthy, but short life for him. I'd miss him, I knew. I'd miss him most of all.

"I don't know what I'll contract," I said, turning the hundred dollar notes in my hands. "I think I'll take my time, listen to the pitches, decide what's best for me and the family."

Mama removed the pot from the stove and waddled to the table. She began to ladle hot porridge into the bowls, starting with Pa's. "You'll do what's best for the family first, young lady. If it works out for you too, then good, but family first," she said, as she plopped a large portion of porridge in my bowl.

I said nothing. I dipped my spoon into the thick, creamy oats and began to swirl them absently.

"What disease do the people in the Compound have, Mama?" Strawberry asked. "I'd like that disease."

Mama guffawed.

"That ain't no disease. Those people are just born rich and lucky. They live up in their nice houses in Eastern Heights, looking down on us carriers, but they need us. We provide their food, and build their fancy houses and make their fancy clothes."

"I heard some of them used to be like us, but they managed to buy their way into the Compound. Not with money, but with deeds," I said quickly.

Mama ladled porridge into Tommy's bowl and then pointed the ladle at me.

"Where did you hear that rubbish?"

"Jillian told me. She heard that —"

"She heard wrong is what she heard. There's no buying your way into the Compound. That's wishful thinking right there. They have the money, we have the diseases. They get our deeds just fine with coin. So get any wishful thinking of buying your way into the Compound out of that head. You just focus on contracting the right disease for this family, missy."

"Yes, Mama," I replied hastily, lowering my eyes to my food.

I'd been watching the Compound from the outside for years. I knew when the Compound gates would open briefly to accept deliveries. I knew all of the spots around Central where you could peek over the Compound walls. Eastern Heights was beautiful. Neat white homes, green parks and gardens, happy people. If there was a way in, I reckoned I'd have as good a chance as any of finding it. And I wouldn't forget my family. Oh no. I'd look after them, but from inside, not out.

But I knew there was no point telling Mama any of that.

I could have walked directly down Main
Street to the Harbourside Disease
Markets, but I turned right on Lincoln
Street and headed towards the Compound
wall. It still took my breath away. It was
made of red brick, stood at least a
hundred feet tall, and ran as far as you
could see — north towards the Harbour
and south to the Yarran Ranges. It
provided a striking contrast to the mud
brick houses of Central.

As I approached the wall, I saw a young
man hunched over a pothole, retching up
hot tar. It hissed and spat as he coughed
the last of it onto the road. Then he picked
up his trowel and began to smooth his
work.

"Morning," I called out to the retcher as
I passed. He wiped some of the tar away
from his mouth with the back of his hand
and gave me a stained smile.

When I reached the wall, I ran my
fingers lightly across the rough bricks,
wondering what it would be like to feel the
wall from the other side. I smiled, then
turned north, keeping to the shadow of
the wall.

The morning was quiet. I only passed one person on my way to the quay — a disfigured mutant with tusks, a thick neck and powerful, stumpy legs. It carried bricks in a sling across its hairy back. I gave it a wave and it grunted in return.

I heard the markets before I saw them — a buzz of excited activity. Then the blue expanse of the Harbour opened out before me, seagulls flocking overhead, a couple of small boats bobbing in the water. Running west, along the docks, snaked a multitude of canvas tents and marquees.

I waded into the crowd and it wasn't long before my interest was piqued by the mouth-watering scents of barbecue. I approached the source of the aroma, a marquee manned by five people with the tumours. One of the infected was standing over a BBQ, roasting a large steak cut freshly from a football sized lump on his thigh. God it smelt good, I thought.

"What about you, miss?" a red headed woman with a fist sized tumour growing from the top of her head asked me. "Are you interested in cooking? Grow what you eat, eat what you grow is our motto. We have a franchise opening up in Southwell."

None of my family had ever contracted the tumours. I was curious.

"How much?" I asked, as I looked first at the redhead, then at the meat. I was hoping they'd offer me a free sample.

"Business is booming at the moment, miss. But we could probably do you a deal for four hundred and fifty dollars."

"Hmm, seems a bit steep," I said, as Mama had instructed.

"A high price for a high earner," the redhead replied. "But, tell you what, you have a nice face and I'm in a good mood. So for you, miss, four hundred and twenty five dollars."

Tumour steaks seemed to be more popular than ever. I'd heard orders from the Compound, in particular, had gone crazy, so I believed you could earn plenty. And yet, it was also one of the most physically repugnant diseases. And Jillian had been telling me recently about rumours of kidnappings and a black market trade in organs. Was it worth the risk?

"I'll think on it," I replied, before moving on.

I next passed three people selling the birthing disease from a domed tent. But I wasn't interested in that, thanks. Mama was doing plenty of birthing for the whole family and we needed money now, not more investments.

I passed the laid-to-waste vendor, but that was no good either. Seeing Pa's deterioration up close had helped me make up my mind. No amount of earnings was worth a disease that ruined your latter years like that.

Next to the laid-to-waste stall was a neat tent selling the mutations.

"Hard to say what your specialty will be before the mutation occurs," said a lean man with elongated, muscular legs, "but we guarantee you'll become something of use — all of us mutants do." He pulled out several black and white sketches. "Here we have our farmers," he said, handing me a picture. I took it and looked down at three lovingly rendered mutants. Each had long tusks that they were using to plough the earth. "Labourers," he said, handing me a second picture that showed a powerfully built creature, short and hunched, hauling timber across its shoulders. "And messengers." The next sketch was of a bunch of creatures like the salesman, each with long, muscular legs that looked like they could run all day.

"Do any of these earn well?" I asked.

He cleared his throat.

"Good honest pay, for honest work," he replied smiling. So no, I thought. "But," he continued quickly, "our disease is one of the few that allows a rich, natural lifespan."

Hmm, well I guess that was appealing. But what good was a long lifespan if you were mutated into a dim-witted cretin who carried mud bricks all of your days? So I thanked him, told him I'd consider it, and then moved on.

I walked past stalls selling the taking disease and nymphomaniacism. I listened to retchers, gas breathers, and leather skins, but none of them appealed. And then, sooner than I had expected, I found myself at the end of the markets. Had I missed something? Why didn't any of the diseases stand out for me like they had for my siblings and parents?

Then, as I turned to wander back the way I had come, I spied an old lady sitting on a stool by herself. She didn't have a stall, but next to her was a sign that read: "True sight infection."

Curious, I approached. She appeared normal. No disfiguration, no obvious signs of illness. She was a tiny woman with thin, white hair; the only ailment she appeared to have was old age. But when she looked up at me, I saw her blue eyes were sharp and lively.

"I've never heard of the true sight infection before," I said.

The old lady smiled, papery skin folding around her mouth.

"It's a rare infection."

"And what does it do?"

"It allows you to see into people and know their true self. It lets you see the things that make them who they are — the important memories, the key moments. It lets you see their fears and desires."

"Ok," I said, not fully understanding. "But how do you earn from that?"

The old crone's grin stretched wider. "It's difficult. Not everyone has the ability to use this disease to their advantage. But for the smart ones that do, they can do very well for themselves."

"I'm sorry, but I need to contract something useful for my family. Unless I can be certain of earning from the infection, I'm not interested." I turned to leave.

"It can get you into the Compound," the old lady called after me. I halted midstride, and then turned slowly. "That is what you want, isn't it? Your one true desire is to get into the Compound, to become one of the elite, to live as they do in a nice white house with clean children playing in a neat garden."

How did she know that? I thought. But of course I knew. She had said it herself. She could see my desires and fears.

"How would your infection help me do that?" I asked, trying to hold onto my suspicions as Mama had taught me. There had to be a con here somewhere.

"There's only one way to get into the Compound as an outsider and that's to be vouched for by a resident. You find the right resident, you look into their heart, you understand what drives them and what they fear, and you use that knowledge to get your invite. At least that's what I did."

"You've been in the Compound?"

"I lived there for fifteen years, up until my James died. After that, I was forced to leave. But I wouldn't trade those fifteen years for anything."

"But how did you … I mean where … I didn't think the residents ever left Eastern Heights."

"They do, but not often. Enough get the itch to see how we live, just like we get the yearning for their life. Tourists. Some move in plain sight, others disguise themselves. But my infection can help you see them clear as day, whether they are disguised or not," she said, tapping her temple softly.

I stared at the old lady for what seemed like an eternity. And the whole time, her perpetual smile never wavered. She had me and she knew it. I sighed.

"How much?" I asked, feeling nervous and giddy at once.

"For you, three hundred and fifty."

I nodded, knowing Mama was going to be furious. But I reached into my pocket and withdrew my money.

The old lady accepted it with a hand that was missing its pinkie and ring finger. I couldn't help but wonder what had happened, but I wasn't allowed to muse for long. After she deposited my money into a small canvas bag, she took my hand in hers and raised it to her lips. She licked my hand from the wrist to the top of my middle finger, her tongue like sandpaper against my skin. I held still, resisting the urge to recoil. Then, suddenly, she placed her wrinkled lips around the tip of my finger and bit it.

I wrenched my hand back, shocked by the sharp pain. My finger was bleeding and there was a drop of blood on the crone's lips. But then, just as quickly, the pain was gone. Whether it was shock or something else, I didn't know. All I knew was that I saw the old woman differently.

She was a wretched creature. Cold, manipulative, despicable. I saw that she had told the truth about her years in the Compound and that she wanted desperately to return. But she knew she never would, which made her bitter and angry. The smile was for show. There was no mirth behind it, just a well-practiced act. And there was something else about her. Something that had been important once. I'd catch a glimpse of it, but then it would recede from view. It was something precious that she had given up to make her deal to enter the Compound. I almost had it when she spoke.

"You're a beautiful girl, with a beautiful, uncorrupted soul. But all things beautiful grow ugly given enough time."

I choked back my disgust, thanked her like Mama had taught me, and then turned and began walking back through the markets.

They didn't look the same anymore. I was shocked to find so many greedy, ugly, and hateful souls. It was overwhelming. As my pulse pounded in my ears, I dropped my eyes to the ground and rushed as quickly as I could through the throng.

Once home, I was relieved to find that the little uns had nice white souls filled with innocent desires about food, hugs and play. Seeing them calmed me a little which, in hindsight, helped me bear the confrontation to come.

"You contracted what?" roared Mama. Mama's true self was a hideous, writhing beast, filled with greed. My heart raced to look at her.

Mama scooped up Lentil in her arms and put him to her breast. He closed his eyes and began to suck contentedly, his true self glowing with delight. Mama's other breast oozed milk, staining her dress.

"The true sight infection," I repeated.

"I never heard of the true sight infection. How do you earn from that?" she demanded.

I took a deep breath, already knowing Mama wouldn't like what I had to say.

"The old lady said I can use it to find a resident of the Compound and get an invite inside. And once I do, I won't forget you and Pa and the little uns. I'll send money out, I swear."

"Ha," Mama said without mirth. "A resident of the Compound indeed. And here I was thinking you kids might listen to your Mama every once in a while. I told you to put such nonsense out of your head."

"The old lady did it. She lived there for fifteen years. She said she used her true sight infection to —"

But Mama wasn't listening. She cut me off.

"More like the waste of time infection. Your Pa gave you good money to contract a disease that would help you pay your way. And you wasted it on a parlour trick and the promise of a happily ever after. I'm just glad he's at work right now so I don't have to see a good man's heart break. I can't believe I gave birth to such a stupid girl," Mama spat. She pulled Lentil off her breast, turned him around, and then pulled her dress down so he could get at the second.

"You know the rules in this family. You don't earn, you look after yourself," she said sharply, her eyes on the infant in her arms. I tried to swallow but couldn't, my mouth was so dry. I could already see what Mama wanted, she wanted me to leave. She birthed us so we could grow up and then earn for the family. Sentimentality ended there for Mama. I blinked hard to force back my tears as Mama turned her icy gaze upon me.

"I want you gone by tomorrow."

"What about Pa," I said quietly, "what will —"

"Don't you worry about Pa. He and I are one on this. You can stay here tonight, but on the morrow you find a way to look after yourself. We can't afford to keep silly girls who waste our money on a worthless disease."

I didn't know how to say goodbye, and I definitely didn't want to face Mama again, so I left before dawn while everyone was still asleep. I didn't take much with me —

the last of my money and a few changes of clothes.

Uncertain what to do next, I wandered, familiarising myself with the effects of my disease. As the sun rose above the horizon, more and more people emerged from their mud brick homes. I was still shocked by the ugly souls I saw, but less so then yesterday. I supposed I was becoming accustomed to the sight. And as I wandered from my house to the Compound wall, to the Harbour and then through Central, I began to see nuances that had not been immediately evident in the aftershock of my contraction.

Not everyone was greedy or angry or hateful. Most people were complex. They displayed a good side and a bad. And the souls themselves differed, I saw. Some were simple, some complex. Some writhed like snakes, some were layered like roses, some were pulsing lights.

I began to realise my sight offered more than just a snapshot of a person. I was soon deciphering the building blocks from which each true self was constructed — the key experiences that made someone who they were. Mistakes, success, love, violence, family, and devastation. I'd catch glimpses of all these things, some clear, others obscured. But each told part of the story of who someone was, and who they were becoming.

Around midday I took my gifts to the Southwell Markets, where the mutant toilers gathered to sell fresh produce and grain along with a few tumour sufferers selling marinated skewers of their flesh. I knew the Compound cart would be loaded in around an hour and I thought that I could talk to the mutant haulers and use my sight to dig out a little information about the residents.

As I strolled through the markets, mutant hawkers hollered in a variety of voices and guttural grunts. Most of the mutants were pleasant to be around. I saw they were generally simpler folk, content with their lives of hard, honest work.

The day was growing hotter, which accentuated the ripe smells of melons, apples, bananas, and pears. Those sweet smells set my empty belly to rumbling. So I bought a shiny red apple from a hunched man with a fulfilled soul and then continued west through the markets.

As I bit into the sweet apple, juice spilling down my chin, I felt like I was almost content in this place. And then, to top it off, I found my resident.

He was sitting on a table wearing a white robe. Behind him stood seven cleans in similar dress. He seemed to have dark hair. I thought he was young. But, to be honest, I found it hard to decipher his physical appearance because I was dazzled by the most beautiful, glowing true self that I had yet seen. It was hard to describe. He was perfect in almost every way. Kind, generous, and loving, with pure motives and matching deeds. And yet I also saw, which confused me greatly, that he was infected. And his key desire was to remain out of the Compound.

My feet took me into the small crowd of diseased that had congregated around the resident. He was speaking to them. To us, I guess.

"A society is not distinct from the people that live in it," he said. "The systems in place, the rules imposed, the sense of community and our place in it are only powerful to the extent that we, the people, accept them.

"Have any of you ever been inside the Compound?" he asked. There were murmurs of no. "And why not?" he continued.

"It's got a big friggin wall for starters," a young, dark haired woman said, drawing laughter from the crowd. The resident smiled.

"But it also has a gate," he said. "Have you ever tried knocking? Or just pushing it open? It's not like it's guarded, is it?"

I saw the woman open her mouth again as if she had thought of something else funny to say, but she stopped, closed it and then shook her head.

"No. You've never tried because you've been brought up with the idea that it is prohibited. But who says? What makes the people out here different to the people in there? Why shouldn't you be allowed to visit the Compound as I am allowed to walk out into Central?"

"What's it like?" I found myself asking.

The young man turned and looked at me, his true self shining brightly, and yet his brow furrowed in concentration and his glowing soul darkened for just a heartbeat. He didn't speak for a time. He just stared, like he knew me. I felt my cheeks redden as he held my gaze. Finally, with an almost imperceptible shake of his head, he spoke again.

"It's very pretty," he answered. "And yet I hate it. Because it's false."

He spoke truly, I saw. He hated the Compound, but why? What did he know that I couldn't see? Every time I'd peeked over the wall it'd looked perfect to me. Heaven next to Central.

The resident turned back to address the wider group.

"Your places as the diseased, mine as the resident, are neither set nor ordained unless we accept them to be so. The system is what we make it. You can survive without earnings. And you can survive without disease. If you wish to try, come with me and I'll show you another way. It's hard work. You'll all labour and you'll all farm and you'll all build and you'll all sew. But you can learn, like I have, and together we can produce enough to subsist happily."

"You said survive without disease," a stunted mutant said.

"Yes. Only one of us needs a disease. I'll take your mutation."

I hadn't expected him to be a taker like Knife. That made even less sense, I thought. But now that he'd said it, I began to notice some of the signs. Elongated eye teeth, black stains around his lips, a bulge on his thigh that might have been a tumour.

"There's always a catch," the mutant said. "How much?"

"I only ask that you give my way a chance. Take the time to learn a skill and then pull your weight in our community. Nothing more."

The crowd erupted into a roar. Some cursed, some laughed, most turned on their heels and wandered back through the markets. But not all of them. Not all of us. I stayed, as did two mutants.

The mutants spoke to the resident first. He talked to them in whispers and soon I saw them nodding. When they were done, two of the nearby cleans led them away from the markets.

Then it was my turn. I didn't know what to say, or what to do, but I stepped closer, drinking in the pureness of his true self. He looked at me again with that uncertain gaze and my stomach fluttered.

"And what disease do you have that you wish me to take?" he asked.

I took a deep breath.

"Actually, I'm happy with my disease."

"Yet curious," the resident said, as he slid from his table onto his feet and took a step towards me, his head tilted slightly to the left. He smelled nice, I thought, like the streets do just after a thunderstorm. Clean and fresh.

"Why would you leave the Compound?" I asked, at which he chuckled. Feeling my cheeks redden, I lowered my gaze.

"No, don't be embarrassed. A pertinent and direct question. I like it. But explaining why is harder than showing. Perhaps you would like to see my community. I think it is far more appealing than the Compound and this city."

I raised my eyes once more and in the dazzling glow of his soul, I saw that he spoke truly. He believed that his community was wonderful. And yet, there was something else. He desperately wanted me to join him there, I saw. But why, I couldn't quite see. I reminded him of someone, or of a particular time in his life, but the experience was from long ago, and was mostly hidden. I couldn't quite untangle it from the rest of him, and that made me more curious if anything.

"No strings attached?" I asked.

"None. A visit only, then you can decide if it is for you or not."

I paused, just like Mama had taught me when negotiating — make them wait. But who was I kidding? I was going to follow this man. Eventually, I bit my lip, nodded. Even if this went nowhere, I rationalized, I could at least use my time to find out a bit more about the Compound from him.

"My name is Lowen," the resident said, holding out a hand to me.

"Fennel," I replied, taking his warm hand in mine.

Lowen lived about an hour's walk from the city — an hour further afield than I'd ever travelled in my life. To be honest, I'd never even contemplated the world existing beyond the city limits. I was surprised by what I found.

It was cooler. Gone was the hot tar, brown buildings and the stink of cohabitation. Instead, I found vast fields of yellowed wheat, rows of green vegetables, and mutants working their land.

It was quiet, and yet I was also assailed by constant noise. I didn't understand how quiet and noise could coexist like that. Long silences were punctuated by insects whirring, birds singing, lizards and field mice scurrying through the plants, and the crunch of gravel under my feet.

After a time, the farms thinned, and then disappeared, replaced with meadows of green grass and yellow flowers, which ran towards the horizon before rising up into undulating hills.

Lowen pointed out his home when we were still a few miles away. It was the only building that marked the landscape for as far as I could see. It was a large, mud brick building, but it was poorly constructed. The western wall was already crumbling in the sun. The roof was thatch, and several spots looked in need of repair. Behind it ran a small creek.

As we turned off the gravel road and onto a dirt path that ran up to the building, I noticed several cleans working in the fields on my left. To my right was a fenced enclosure housing a number of strange, white animals that I had never seen before.

"They're called sheep," Lowen said as we passed them.

"And what do you do with them?" I asked.

"They provide us with wool for our garments, and milk and meat."

"You eat animals," I responded, part horrified, part bemused. The idea had never occurred to me. Lowen laughed.

There were about twenty people working and living in the community. Other than Lowen and the three of us diseased that had followed him home that day, they were all clean.

"This is Robin," Lowen said, introducing me to a girl a few years older than myself. She was short, very slight of build, and she smiled broadly. "Robin joined us a few months ago and she's currently learning how to weave and sew. We make our own clothes and blankets, and trade excess in town for the things we can't yet grow ourselves."

"Nice to meet you," Robin said. Robin's true self showed her as grateful, happy, hopeful, but there were also some scars there, past experiences that had hardened her, and that she was working to forget.

"What if you don't like it?" I blurted out. Lowen chuckled, but urged me to continue. "What if it's too hard, or you miss home or ... I don't know, you just get sick of sewing and want to leave?"

"Then I can go," Robin said, looking to Lowen.

"This isn't a prison, Fennel," he said. "Robin has the same deal as everyone else. I took her disease, and she tries to live clean while she learns the skills needed to survive out here. But no one is keeping her here. Anyone who wants to return to the city, can."

"And has anyone ever left?"

Lowen smiled.

"I'm sure there've been times when people have thought about it. But so far, no one has actually left. They're sticking it out, giving the work a go."

I must have looked doubtful, because Lowen quickly continued.

"It's hard to understand unless you experience it, Fennel," he said. "How about you let Robin show you around tomorrow? She can take you to her classes so you can try things first hand. What do you say?"

I hesitated, looking from Robin, to Lowen, then back again.

"It's not so hard learning to sew," Robin said, smiling. "It just takes a little practice."

I took a breath.

"Ok."

"Great. I'll meet you first thing tomorrow," she said, and soon after she was walking back to the building.

"So, I guess this means you're staying with us," Lowen said.

When I glanced across at him, I saw his heart radiated gold light. At that moment, as a smile danced on his lips and in his eyes, there was nothing more I wanted to do than please him by saying I would stay for good. But that wouldn't be the truth, I knew. I rubbed my fingertips together. They could still feel the rough brick wall of the Compound. I wasn't certain Lowen could or would help me and yet...

"I'll stay for a little while," I said.

The following morning, I sat in the main hall on a mat on the floor, Robin beside me. The trestle tables that were used for meals had been pushed against the walls, the chairs stacked neatly beside them.

Other cleans sat in groups around the hall, like Robin and I. Some sewed, others were peeling vegetables for lunch. Still others were twisting white wool into yarn. Wool that was apparently cut straight from the backs of the sheep out in the paddocks.

Robin was watching intently as I pushed my needle once more through the piece of cloth.

"Good," she said. "Now pull the thread until the stitch is tight."

I did as instructed, the thread making a *whisk* sound. I flipped the material over and looked down at my work. The stitches weren't as neat or as evenly spaced as Robin's, and there was a dot of red in the middle where I'd pricked my finger, but I felt a smile forcing its way to my lips.

"You're a natural, Fennel," Robin said.

When I looked up, I saw her true self filling with pride, in me, her student.

"How did you end up here, Robin?" I asked.

"Same as most people, I guess," she said, turning her attention back to her own sewing. But she wanted to talk, I saw.

"What did you give up?"

"Nymphomaniacism. Before I met Lowen I sold myself in Collins Street."

I looked away from her, embarrassed. I'd never been to the nympho district, but I knew of it. Everybody knew of it. It was good money, it was said.

"I'm sorry."

"No need to be sorry. Lowen saved me," she said. But I was sorry. Because I could see her essence darkening, stained by the memories of despair and dread that she had carried with her in that past life. That she carried still, deep down.

"After my sixteenth name day, I worked the street. It was hard and easy. Hard up here," she said, stopping her work to point to her temple, "because the disease made it easy, made me want to do it, even when I didn't like it, even when I ... even when I began to not like me." She swallowed, eyes down, leaving me to wonder just how bad it had got for her before Lowen came along. I suddenly didn't want to look at her to find out, so I glanced away. She cleared her throat and continued.

"Anyway, I was there around six years before Lowen found me. He told me what he was doing and what he was offering. I didn't think on it for long. I'd been dreaming of an out for a long time, and he brought me a better one than I'd ever contemplated. I came home with him and, well, here I still am."

I looked back at her, her true self lightening as her thoughts turned to Lowen.

"He's quite compelling, isn't he?" I said.

She smiled, bashful, before looking up at me.

"Yes, he is."

Just then, the main doors opened and Lowen entered the hall, all eyes turning towards him. He stood at the edge of the room, searching for a moment until he looked in our direction. Then he was smiling, and approaching quickly.

"We've got a master seamstress in the making here, Lowan," Robin said. I felt my cheeks redden.

"I see," he said, stopping next to us, looking down at my work. "May I?" He held out a hand and I gave him the material. He studied it carefully, as if admiring a work of great art. Then he nodded and handed it back.

"You have a real knack for sewing, Fennel." Then he turned to Robin. "Do you mind if I borrow your student for a while?"

"Not at all," Robin said. "We were due a break."

The sun beat warmly on my back as Lowen led me away from the hall towards fields which emitted a sweet, loamy aroma. The air around me hummed with the drone of bees flying to and fro. A steady clack, clack, clack rang out from near the road where one of the cleans was using a large mallet to hammer a fence post into the ground.

Lowen stopped just shy of a bed of cabbages. Three cleans were hunched down in various spots, pulling weeds from the rows.

Lowen dropped to his haunches and pulled a weed from between two plants. He tossed it casually aside.

"It looks like hard work," I said, just to fill the silence.

Lowen looked up at me and smiled.

"It is. Very hard. But until you've eaten something you've grown yourself, it's difficult to explain how satisfying hard work can be."

I nodded as if I understood. But I didn't. I got that doing something yourself could give some brief satisfaction, like my sewing, but would that feeling last long enough to warrant giving up all of the conveniences of city life? I wasn't so sure. Standing again, Lowen dusted his hands against each other.

"Tell me about your disease, Fennel," he said.

"I've contracted the true sight infection."

"I don't think I've heard of that before. What are the effects?"

"It allows me to see people truly. Who they are and what they desire."

"Hmm. And what do you see in me?"

I looked at him for a while before answering.

"You're a very, very good man, Lowen," I said.

"Thank you for saying so. What else?"

"I see that you believe in your community, that you consider that this is the true purpose of your life. And ..."

"And what?"

I hesitated, looking again at his hatred of the Compound.

"Why don't you want to return to the Compound?" I asked before I lost the nerve. And as I did, his brow furrowed and, just behind the whiteness of his true self, I saw something darker, something which almost revealed itself, but then slunk away, leaving gold and white.

"You seem to have a fascination with my old home," Lowen said. I didn't deny it. I didn't say anything.

Lowen sighed. "Appearances can be deceiving, Fennel. Particularly when those appearances are manufactured to instil envy and separation.

"What do you know of the origin of diseases?" he asked.

"There's always been disease, hasn't there?"

"Yes and no. Yes, they've always existed. But their willing contraction and exploitation, that's much more recent."

Lowen looked off into the distance, hands twisting within each other as he gathered his thoughts. Finally, he continued.

"Once, those living in Central were not much different to those in Eastern Heights. This was before the wall.

"Eastern Heights always had nicer houses, but anyone could buy one if they had the money. And the way you earned money was to work hard, to be the most skilful builder or artisan or chef. And importantly, back then, anyone could learn those skills.

"After a while though, a group of proud, old families with money — like my own — decided that this 'new money' was not something they wanted to associate with. They didn't like the constant expansion of the elite. And so they came up with an idea. The old families began

convincing people in Central that the
hardest workers were mutants. That the
best clothing wasn't sewn, it was
harvested from a leather skin. That the
best meat wasn't from sheep, but from
tumour sufferers. And as the old families
paid for these services, the inhabitants of
Central began to contract the diseases
sought after by those with the money."

"Only someone who grew up in the
Compound, who's never gone without
food, would think that was a terrible
trade," I blurted out, seeing his true self
anger as I spoke the words. I swallowed,
watching him wrestle with his beliefs and
the realisation that his upbringing might
have left him devoid of the life experience
of the people he was trying to save.
Eventually, the anger dissipated, the
white and gold returned. He nodded.

"Ok," he said. "Perhaps I can
understand why the poor bought into this
system. Perhaps. But the residents could
have shared their wealth in other ways.
Instead, they created a new class of
worker. Workers who would never be like
them. Because old money was clean. New
money was diseased. And that's why you
can only look into the Compound from
afar. They created a system that makes

you different. The wall just punctuated the declaration."

I looked down at my feet, shuffling in the dirt, watching it form little brown waves that washed over the toes of my shoes.

"But you could change all of that," I said quietly. "You could vouch for me, for all of us, to come back with you."

He stared at me then, emotions chasing themselves across his face — shock, confusion, dismay.

"That wouldn't be change, Fennel."

"So you've never even thought of going home? Don't you still have family there? Friends?"

"No."

I saw he was lying.

"So nothing could make you return?"

He hesitated, looking out over the workers.

"Right now, there's nothing I can envisage that would make me go back. But I'd be naive to say things will never change. Sometimes life steers you towards doing something you don't want to do."

I wasn't certain he was still talking about the future.

"You know, your disease," he said, turning back to me, changing tack. "I don't think you need it."

"Oh really, why's that?" I said, bemused.

"You don't need a disease to see the true self of someone. You just get to know them. At least that's what I do."

The following day, Lowen left for the city with a cohort of cleans, including Robin. He entrusted me to a man called Thomas, the first person who'd agreed to give Lowen his disease.

Thomas' true self was different to Lowen. To Robin as well for that matter. It wasn't imbued with hope, it was just neutral. Neither good, nor bad. Resigned to the fact that this was his life now, and a realisation that this might be as good as it got for him.

We spent the day together weeding vegetable crops. It was monotonous, back breaking work. Down on our knees pulling weeds from rows, being careful not to crush the carrots, cabbages, or whatever other plant we were working between. Within an hour I was sweating, aching and ready to throw it in. But I didn't. I made myself go on. Trying to understand why anyone would do this day in, day out.

"It's better than the pain," Thomas answered when I put the query to him. "Those hawkers in the disease markets never mention it when they're selling the diseases, but most infections bring suffering at one point or another."

"What did you have?"

"The tumours. They were uncomfortable to carry, and they hurt like a bastard when you sliced them. Not as bad as some diseases, but it built up on you. Got so I hated the idea of cooking, of someone approaching my BBQ. But then Lowen did, and he had a different proposal for me."

I shuffled forward, grunting as I shifted position, yanking at another weed and tossing it behind me.

"But let me ask you this. How many hours a day would you have had to cook for to earn enough to survive back in the city? Compared to this, I mean?"

"Oh, I don't know," he said, stopping to wipe his brow and squint up at the cloud mottled sky. "Probably a couple of hours a day and I'd earn enough to eat and pay the rent. Another hour and I could afford a few luxuries."

"And two, three hours of that was worse than ten hours here doing this?"

He looked across at me and just shrugged. But his true self wasn't quite as nonchalant. He'd had similar thoughts, I saw. Memories of pain faded over time, and he'd sometimes wondered if it had all been as bad as he liked to say.

"I'm not going to lie. I've wanted to go back at times, but I never have."

"Why not?"

"Lowen, mainly. Maybe the pain back there isn't that much worse than the hard life here. Maybe. But I've never known anyone in the city willing to give me as much as Lowen has. And it's not just him taking my disease. It's the time he gives to me, his interest in me as a person. God, sometimes I think he even likes me. No one before Lowen ever made me feel like I might be a better person than I was. Not my Mama, not my ex-wife. No one. I stay for that feeling as much as anything. For a little of Lowen's glow to rub off on me from time to time."

He turned his back on me and hopped over a row of plants, plucking at the ground again.

"Why do you think he did it? Leaving the Compound to begin taking diseases that is?"

For a long time there was silence.

"Don't know," Thomas eventually said without turning back to look at me.

"Aren't you curious?"

"Yep. But Lowen doesn't want to talk about it, so I don't push him. Whatever the reasons, I expect they're personal and none of my damn business."

Which wasn't a good enough answer for me.

"Do you miss it?" I asked Lowen as we walked beside the creek that burbled quietly, whispering to itself.

Friday was a day of rest for the community. I'd been preparing to spend mine in bed, give my aching muscles and raw fingers a chance to recover. But Lowen wouldn't have any of that and so, instead, here I was, forcing movement into my sore body.

"Miss what?" Lowen asked, his true self growing opaque.

The Compound, I wanted to say. *Your neat house, your family.*

"Being clean," I tried instead. I watched him relax again, his essence becoming white, slightly translucent, flowing like the creek.

"Yes, I miss that. Sometimes. But then I remind myself what my disease is achieving."

"Hmm," I said, trying to fight the smirk forming at the corners of my mouth. I didn't succeed, not completely. Lowen saw me smile.

"What?"

"It's just you've been trying to convince me to give up this disease of mine and join the community and, well, here you are spruiking the benefits of your own affliction."

Lowen chuckled, a light throaty guffaw.

"I see. Well, we're all allowed our contradictions, aren't we?"

"I guess," I said, continuing to walk. A breeze erupted from across the stream, poking at the water and blitzing my hair. I brushed my fringe out of my eyes and turned to see Lowen glancing at me, but he turned away quickly as I caught him.

"What about you?" Lowen asked, staring ahead, like he was intentionally avoiding my gaze. "Do you miss being clean?"

I walked for a while, thinking, not exactly sure of my answer until my mouth opened and the words began to spill out.

"Yes and no. Meeting you, meeting Robin, it's nice seeing just how good people can be. On the other hand, it didn't bring me much joy to see how many truly greedy, sad and evil people there were in the city. But if I gave it up, it'd feel like I was just putting my head in the sand and pretending everything was right with the world. I don't know. Part of me wishes I didn't know people could be so bad. Part knows that this disease has opened my eyes to the real world."

"Hmm, the real world," Lowen muttered.

"What?"

"Nothing. It's just the way you talk of the Compound ... You haven't actually seen any residents since contracting your disease, have you?"

"I've seen you."

But I knew that wasn't what he was getting at. I sighed.

"You really believe the residents are despicable, don't you?" I said.

"I know they are. It was better to start again than try and change the lives in there."

"You seem ok," I said, shrugging, smiling.

It was meant to be light hearted but, behind his white soul, I saw a flicker of something black responding to my words. Then Lowen was turning from me and walking ahead, quickly. What had I said? I hurried to catch up with him and then I fell in step alongside. We walked in silence for a while.

"Can I ask you," Lowen said after a time, "how you were intending to survive with your disease? How would you earn?"

From tricking a resident into taking me back, I thought. *Someone like you.*

"I was told if you could discover what someone wants then you could be rewarded for helping them achieve their desire."

Lowen stopped suddenly, his true self lightening again, and then he bent over and splashed some of the creek water into his face. He stood again and turned to look at me.

"What do I want? Right now?" he asked.

I looked at him. I could see his desire to swim, to splash, to cool down in the shallows of the stream.

"You want to bathe."

"And why would I need your gift to help me achieve that?"

I frowned. That wasn't what the old lady meant. Nor was it what I meant.

"I ... I guess ..."

But then he reached down and splashed me with water. And I squealed and frowned and smiled. It felt so cold, and yet good, like I was alive. And soon I was rushing into the stream and kicking water at him. Like a kid. Like we were both kids. Who didn't care what our Mama's would say when we came back cold and wet and dripping.

Walking back to the community, our gowns soaked, smiles still on our faces, I looked at Lowen again and saw his true self buzzing. He was happy. And part of that happiness, I saw, was being with me.

My days continued like that for a while. Sewing garments, pulling weeds, peeling vegetables. My fingers grew calloused, my body began slowly to adjust. I was still bone tired when I'd lay my head down each night, but the aches were less.

Lowen would often seek me out at meal times. And on Fridays we'd go walking for half an hour here, an hour there, whatever he could spare away from his responsibilities.

When I was with him, the community was nice. I could almost forget the drudgery of the work, the repetition, the boredom. I liked our walks. I liked our discussions. Most of all, I enjoyed our arguments about the city and our debates on how life should be lived. What that said about me, I wasn't quite sure.

But then, they'd be over. And I'd go back to sewing, or weeding, or digging. And Lowen would go to town to recruit. Sometimes for a day. Sometimes for a few. And when that happened, my mind would wander. I mean, what else could I do? The work was hardly intellectually stimulating. And by the end of those days I'd have grown tired of it all. I'd despise the place and what I had to do to contribute to the community. And in those moments I'd find myself thinking about my family, and the city, and the wall, and what was waiting for me on the other side of it.

Eventually, I began to realise that nothing had changed inside me, really, despite Lowen's best efforts. I didn't see myself in need of saving like the others did. And I didn't see the same kind of beauty out here that Lowen saw. Or if I did, it was fleeting, and I also saw the hard work as just hard work. And my desire to live more easily back in the city, in the Compound, remained.

I needed to go home, I realised. The surprise in that thought was the sadness that accompanied it.

"What do you want in life, Fennel?" Lowen asked me. I sat across from him at the long table, a bowl of potato soup before me, its earthy scent making my mouth water. I'd miss the food, I knew. It was one thing the community did really well.

I looked up from my bowl and spied something new in his true self. I didn't understand it at first.

"I don't know," I said absently. I dipped my spoon into the soup and then raised it to my mouth. It was warm and creamy with just a hint of smokiness. Delicious.

"You've seen what we can offer here, now. I feel like a choice is nearly upon you. Have you had any thoughts on what you will do? Is this life something you could buy into?"

I looked back at him and, yes, there was something new. Concern? Maybe. Warmness? Yes. And, *oh,* I thought. It was affection. For me. I felt myself blushing and looked away.

"What do you want me to do?" I asked, glancing back at him, my heart racing.

I watched him mull the question over. I watched his affection grow. But there was a nervousness there. This was very important to him, I saw.

"I want you to give me your disease and then stay here with us. With me."

But I didn't want that. What I wanted was for Lowen to take me back home. Back to his real home.

And then I recalled some of his past words. He'd once said that he could never rule out something cropping up in life that would lead him back to the Compound. Could that something be me?

Maybe this was the opportunity the old lady had been talking about. Find a resident, determine his desires and use them. I was Lowen's desire. Rescuing me was something he needed to do. So what if I gave him what he wanted? Gave him my gift to see truly? Wouldn't he then see me like I'd seen him? And once he saw how much I needed the Compound, that it wasn't just fantasies and words, that it was something deeper, in the core of me, well, how could he refuse to take me then if he truly cared?

"Ok," I replied, watching the shock etch his features.

It was gentler than the giving of the true sight.

Lowen led me to the sleeping quarters, which we had to ourselves while the others ate. We sat amongst the bedrolls and faced each other. A crude wall hid us from the common room.

Lowen gave me a gentle kiss and then, with an exchange of breath, I saw him. Not his true self, his physical self. To my shame, my impulse was revulsion.

The golden glow of his beautiful soul no longer obfuscated the tumours that riddled the right side of his face. Nor the black tar that slid unwanted from his mouth. Nor the tusk that poked through his left cheek. Nor the hair on his arms, nor the hunch of his back, nor the rancid smell of his rotting feet. I fought against my urge to retch and forced a smile to my face hoping it didn't look like a grimace.

With rheumy eyes, he looked me up and down.

"I see you truly, Fennel," he said.

"And?" I asked.

He hesitated, and then tears budded in his eyes. He cleared his throat, blinking hard.

"There's nothing for you here. Not now, anyway," he croaked, looking away, like he was ashamed of me. Like I'd failed him somehow. Or he'd failed me.

"But, but," I stammered, "but you care for me."

"I do," he said, eyes still averted. A tear rolled down his cheek. "Too much to give you what you want. I can't take you to the Compound."

"But it's your home —"

"This is my home," he cut me off.

I sat there stunned. I wanted to scream. I wanted to demand that he give me what I wanted. But who was I kidding? My plan, if you could even call it that, involved little more than the fancy of a young girl deluding herself that she could be clever. I'd gambled and lost. Lowan would never help me achieve my true desire. And I hated him for that. I hated this place and these crazy people.

Without a word, my rage simmering under a stony exterior, I rose to my feet and left.

It wasn't long before I was back in amongst the heat and noise of the city. It was familiar and yet strange. Like I had immersed myself within a distorted reflection of the place I'd grown up in.

The stench of civilisation assaulted me wherever I went. And people. Everywhere. The sick and diseased jostling, bumping, crowding me. To escape them, at least temporarily, I sought out Western Park. I'd frequented it often when I was younger. It held peace, a little green, and, most importantly, a small hill from which I could just see over a low section of the Compound wall.

I arrived on dusk. It was as I remembered — the copse of elms and oaks, the wide lawns smattered with leaves, a central pond. And dominating the scenery was the red Compound wall. I felt a little gladder to see it. And yet it seemed more distant than ever before now that I'd given up my disease. How had I been so stupid?

I scaled the hill at the far end of the park, reaching the top just as the last of the sun sank below the horizon. I stood, looking over the wall at the tops of the white houses, watching the gas lamps come on like blinking stars as daylight leaked from the world. Finally, when the last of the sunlight was gone and I was left in darkness, when I could see no more of paradise, I sat down on the grass to take stock, removing the last of my money from my pack.

One hundred and forty-nine dollars. I counted it again to be sure. It wasn't enough, I knew. I couldn't start again with that. It wouldn't even be enough to afford the mutations. I sighed, realising I only had one option left. One chance at making something of the mess I'd created for myself.

I stuffed my money back in my pack, and I left the park. I headed south towards the foot of the Yarran ranges, to the edge of Southwell, where the wealthy diseased lived in new homes neatly rendered with dark mud. This was where the takers plied their trade.

I'd only visited once before, but I found the house easily enough. It was at the end of Rosen Street, small for this area, but neat.

I took a deep breath as I approached the front door, and then knocked, suddenly nervous that he wouldn't answer, or that he would and he'd turn me away. I realised I was holding my breath. I exhaled. And then there were the sounds of soft footsteps approaching the door from the inside. And before I could think of what I would say, the door clicked, and was opening. I was met with a look of suspicion, which quickly dissolved into surprise.

"Fennel?" my brother said. I noticed he had a hint of fur poking out from under his collar, and slightly elongated front teeth.

"Hello, Knife."

After I'd told him everything, I waited for Knife to respond. He sat across the wooden table from me, his brow furrowed, his mouth a silent frown.

I took a sip of my tea, grimacing as I realised it had long grown cold. I placed the cup back on the table with a soft clink, and then looked around Knife's kitchen.

The stove was new and clean. It looked like it had rarely been lit. The crockery on the shelves appeared to be for decoration only. I doubt he ate here very often, but I guess he could afford not to. The kitchen opened into a lounge room. A couple of leather couches faced an empty, blackened fireplace.

"So, you want my help, I suppose," Knife said, drawing my attention again.

"No … I mean, I guess."

He sighed.

"And why should I help you, Fennel? You got yourself into this mess. You picked a disease I've never heard of and then you gave it up. Why? What did Mama teach you?"

I swallowed, trying to force back the lump in my throat.

"I'm sorry, okay? I just … I just don't know what to do."

He sighed again.

"How much money have you got left?"

"One hundred and forty-nine dollars."

He shook his head.

"I'm such a soft touch," he mumbled to himself, pushing his chair back and rising from the table. I watched him walk into the kitchen and reach under the bench where he withdrew a ceramic jar.

"I'll spot you the cost of a disease," he said, removing the lid from the jar and reaching inside.

"I want to get my true sight infection back. It only cost —"

"A useful disease," he said, cutting me off. "You wasted money once. You aren't wasting mine, okay?"

He stared at me until I looked away. And then I felt my head nodding as I blinked back the tears.

"A friend of mine, Majoris, she trades in leather skins and she's after a new recruit. I'll talk to her tomorrow about a contraction. You can work for her for a while, earn enough to pay me back and then find a place of your own."

I hesitated, swallowing. Of all the diseased, leather skins were the most hideous. More so than mutants, worse than tumour sufferers. I wanted to refuse, I wanted to argue for something better. But I didn't. What choice did I really have? I turned back to Knife and nodded again. He thrust some bills at me, which I accepted, tentatively. I felt the tears then, hot on my cheeks and salty at the corners of my mouth.

Knife's hand was suddenly under my chin, lifting my face to look at him. He wasn't angry anymore, he was just my brother.

"You're really obsessed with this Compound thing, aren't you? Always have been, I guess."

I shrugged. What could I say?

He sighed again.

"Majoris, well, there's something else about her. She sells to the Compound. Her girls get to visit for the harvesting."

A smile must have broken out across my face then, because he smiled too.

"Now don't start getting silly ideas. It isn't what you wanted. You won't get to stay long. But it's the best I can do for you."

When I threw my arms around him and squeezed he stiffened at first, but then he relaxed and returned my embrace. After a while, he pulled back from me, holding me gently at arm's length.

"You can stay here till you find your feet. But it's time to grow up now, Fennel. Time to be responsible. Time to make your own way in the world like the rest of us."

Majoris was a woman in her fifties with brown hair, flecked with grey. Her neck and arms were covered in scars. I presumed they continued under her black tunic, across her chest and back.

She'd been a leather skin most of her life, she told me, but she was clean now. One of my brother's clients. Contracts with the Compound can change a fortune like that. She'd done her time, sold her skin and now, well, others worked for her.

She gave me a good deal, at least that's what Knife said. It was four hundred and fifty dollars for the contraction, and Majoris agreed that any future profits would be split between us sixty, forty — my share being the forty. As I paid the upfront fee, encouraged by Knife, I couldn't help but feel that I was handing over a part of myself to this stranger.

When the transaction was done, Majoris brought one of her girls in from outside. She was short and frumpy, her face tan and rough. Beneath her tunic were misshapen bulges where the excess skin was forming. I tried not to see me in that girl. I tried not to shudder as she pricked my finger and mixed her blood with mine.

"Four weeks," Majoris said, when the girl was done. "I'll be back then to inspect the harvest." She tossed me a small jar containing a pearl coloured, translucent gel. "Rub that into your back, belly and legs when the disease takes hold. It'll keep your skin soft."

I nodded, but couldn't find any words.

"Thank you, Majoris," Knife said on my behalf. "I'll make sure she's ready when you return."

The skin on my belly began to change first. It darkened in colour, and hardened until it didn't feel like me, until it was puckered, and foreign. I applied the gel Majoris had given me to keep the skin supple.

My back followed next. And then my arms, legs, my neck and face. And once the constitution of my epidermis had altered, it began growing.

I watched in horrid fascination as the skin of my belly loosened, bunched, then sagged. It was separating from the fat and muscles beneath, becoming a flesh blanket that folded back on itself. And still it grew bigger, longer, until the skin hung to my waist, then my thighs, my knees. My back followed trend, loosening, expanding, sagging.

I continued to apply the gel, but it became more difficult and time consuming as I had to work my way between folds of the hardened skin.

It was still me under it all, I told myself. But I didn't feel the same. I stopped going outside because, when I did, all I got was stares from passers-by. But even staying locked up in Knife's house didn't protect me from the realisation of what I'd become. Knife tried hard, but he couldn't completely hide the flickers of disgust that flashed across his face when he saw me.

So I kept to myself, I grew, I applied my cream. And as my skin expanded, so did an emptiness inside of me. Would I adjust eventually? I wondered. Would I learn to cope with my new life, my new self? I expected I had too. Everyone else did. And the Compound. I was going to get inside the Compound. It was that thought that kept me going.

Finally, my body having changed, my skin ready, I stood with Majoris outside the Compound gates waiting to be admitted. My stomach roiled and twisted, excited to go inside, nervous about what was to come.

It was just on dusk, but I was still hot under the girdle Majoris had given me to wear beneath my tunic. It allowed me to walk without tripping, as she said it would.

The gates clicked, and then swung inward. My heart accelerated, the sound of it loud in my ears as I took in what I'd longed to see.

The Compound was stunning. The tarred roads of Central ended at the wall, fading into wide, cobbled streets. There were footpaths, and gas lamps creating small pools of illumination. There was grass, and gardens — red and white roses contrasting with dark green foliage. And of course the houses — immaculate, white buildings that lined the streets.

I tried to consume every detail so I could return here in my mind, over and over, after my visit was done. But Majoris didn't allow me to dwell on the scenery for long.

"This is Miss Constrine, my most important client," she said, guiding me inside the gate.

Miss Constrine was tall, with pale skin and a sharp, angular face. Her dark hair was pulled back so tight it looked painful. She wore black leather, I saw.

"Pleased to meet you, ma'am," I said, remembering the manners Mama had taught me.

"Hmm," Miss Constrine said, as if I hadn't spoken. She began to circle me slowly. "Yes, it will do, I think. Very nice. The light colouring, good skin." I stood still as she walked around me. She completed her loop and then stopped, staring at me as if appraising chattels. I suddenly felt self-conscious, unsure of how to hold myself. I felt inferior in this woman's eyes and, unbidden, I recalled how Lowen had always looked at me and realised this resident was nothing like him.

"Come," she demanded. She turned and walked up the cobbled street. Majoris took my arm in hand and led me after her. I wasn't sure I would have voluntarily followed without Majoris' cajoling.

Miss Constrine led us into the yard of a nearby house decorated with elaborate columns. Large, dark windows looked down on me, like the black eyes of some monster. I wondered why there were no lights burning, but I soon realised we weren't heading inside.

I followed Miss Constrine around the back of the home, where there was a second building. It was rendered white like the main house, but the building was small and flat. Barely a room, really. It had no windows, which I thought odd, but a large door was wide open, warm light spilling out.

As I walked inside, my heart beat harder, and I began to feel nauseous. The floor was cement, sloping to a long grate at the back of the room. In the middle stood a large metal table with four cuffs for hands and legs. A smaller metal table, covered in implements, was close by. The room had the faint scent of ammonia.

"This way," Majoris urged, guiding me to the table. My legs were stiff. They felt foreign as I moved. *I'm in the Compound,* I reminded myself. But it no longer seemed important.

Majoris helped me undress as Miss Constrine began inspecting the scalpels, scrapers, and other metal instruments. Eventually, she turned to survey me.

Her gaze across my naked flesh was piercing, appraising. I wondered what I would have seen of her if I still had my true sight. Not the beauty of the Compound gardens, I thought. Not the whiteness of the houses.

"It's ok," Majoris whispered to me. In her eyes I saw understanding. It'd been her on this table years before. "Miss Constrine is a professional. This will be done very quickly. Now, please, lay down on the table."

I looked at it. It was immense. And reflected in its sterile surface was a distorted reflection of my face, frowning, eyes darting to and fro looking for someone to save me. But no one did.

I climbed onto the cold table and lay face down, trembling. Majoris clipped my wrists and ankles into the cuffs. I closed my eyes, willing this to be over as soon as possible.

Miss Constrine was near now, leaning over me. I felt her gaze boring into the back of my head, and then her cold touch in the folds of the skin of my back.

My breathing grew harsh. I could feel it bouncing back from the surface of the table, warm against my cheeks. My body was tense. I knew what was coming, and yet, I knew I didn't really know.

And then it began.

There was an electric pinch high up towards my right shoulder blade, and then it was moving quickly to my left, followed by what felt like a burning hot coal being dragged across my back. I screamed. I couldn't help it.

The skin on my back was wrenched, and I heard tearing, felt the warm blood rolling over my sides, and I screamed again as my back caught alight, fire flickering over the top half. The electric pinch of the scalpel was back, just above my buttocks. I bucked hard, but the restraints held me in place.

There was a clatter as the scalpel was dropped into a tray. I could hear Miss Constrine grabbing another instrument.

Something stabbed my right side then, like a punch in the ribs. I groaned, tears streaming down my face, pooling on the table in front of me.

And then something metal, foreign, was forced into me, under the skin, and worked back and forth, slicing at my nerve endings like someone prodding a rotten tooth. I bucked again, hard, trying to escape the pain. I was on fire, and I could taste copper in my mouth where I'd bitten my tongue. My own screams reverberated around the room.

I couldn't stand this anymore. I wanted the agony to end, God I wanted it to stop. My flesh burned as I felt it all coming loose, being cut and pulled from me as I wailed and wailed and then, thankfully, the world faded, replaced with blackness.

I awoke back in my bed in Knife's house, lying on my side. My body hummed with pain, throbbing. I tried to move, but my back and stomach screamed in protest and I inhaled sharply, my vision jolting as I settled back into the uncomfortable position I'd been left in. I swallowed, took a deep breath, cold sweat beading on my forehead. My throat was parched.

"Knife," I croaked. "Knife."

At first I wondered if he was even at home, the house being so quiet. But then he was standing in the doorway, a glass of water in his hands.

"Hey," he said. He approached, dropped to his knees, and then he awkwardly held the glass to my lips so that I could sip a little coolness into my mouth.

"How did I get here?" I asked when I was done.

"A couple of residents helped Majoris get you back. She applied a poultice to your wounds. You're to leave it on for the next couple of weeks."

I adjusted my head to look at my belly and could see the padding under my tunic. It felt moist. A coolness dousing just the tip of the steady throb of pain that encased me.

"Okay."

"She left your money here. A pretty good haul, three hundred and fifty."

I winced. "Take it. And take the other hundred I owe you from my pack."

He looked at me for a while, then nodded.

"You did good, you know? And it'll get easier. The diseases always do. I took a while to adjust to mine as well. But I learned, as you will. We all have to bear our diseases, the good and the bad," Knife said, repeating Mama's words.

"Do we?" I asked before thinking.

Knife inhaled. I thought he was going to say something reassuring. Something to make me appreciate my new life more. Something that would inspire me.

"Eight weeks, Majoris said. You'll be healed and ready for another harvest then."

My eyes felt hot, and I blinked hard, but a tear escaped anyway and began to roll down my cheek.

"Don't worry, you can stay here till then. After that, you can look for your own place, hey?"

He rose back to his feet and went to the door.

"Why do we have to suffer to earn?" I asked, stopping him halfway out of the room. He turned slowly, looking over at me.

"It is what it is, Fennel. As it always has been. And always will be."

But I wasn't so sure anymore.

It was a week before I got out of bed, two before I could move freely around the house. The pain receded slowly, as Knife said it would. And as my wounds healed, I began to feel more like my old self. Because my skin wasn't growing yet, and I was almost pain free.

If I was to operate on eight week cycles, this was the sweet spot, I realised. This was my window to be me.

The day I left the house, I headed first to the Compound wall, running my fingers lightly against its rough, red surface. I saw the white houses, in my mind, the cobble stoned streets, the gas lamps and gardens. And then I saw the table, Miss Constrine's glare, my terrified reflection clouding with hot breath. I pulled my hand back sharply, shaking my head.

I wandered Central, re-familiarising myself with the town. I had lunch at the harbour, watching birds glide out over the sea.

At two o'clock, I staked out the Compound gates. I saw two mutants admitted to deliver a cart of grain. And as one wandered away from the cart, just slightly, he was quickly surrounded by three large residents, imposing themselves, pointing, cursing, herding the mutant back towards his cart and out the gate. And I felt strange watching the display, the ugly bravado. What did they think he was going to do? Suddenly disappear into the Compound never to be found again?

Afterwards, I found myself back at the entrance to the Southwell Markets. There was a risk of finding Lowen here, I knew. I didn't know how I would feel about that, or what I would say. And yet a small part of me hoped I'd see him again. So I immersed myself in the crowd, inhaling the scents of fresh fruit, losing myself amongst the cries and pitches of the mutant hawkers. It was nice being back.

I made my way to the end of the markets, needing to see if the community were preaching today. And they were.

Robin, who I'd last seen holding needle and thread, sat on a table, some familiar people in white robes standing behind her. She was offering to take diseases from those that had gathered around her.

Where was Lowen, though? I didn't understand what had happened.

I joined the crowd and listened to Robin's spiel. She spoke kindly, she spoke well, but she was no Lowen.

After everyone had finished laughing and cursing and had wandered off, I approached her cautiously, nervously. The disease had darkened my skin, hardened my cheeks, but she recognised me and met me with a smile and a hug. I winced as she squeezed, my body still tender.

"Fennel, it's so amazing to see you. How are you?"

"Good, I'm good," I lied, pulling back from her. "So you take diseases now too?"

Her face grew grave.

"Yes. I have to. Lowen's no longer well enough to recruit, I'm afraid. He doesn't have much time left. But we're making sure his good work will continue."

"Oh," was all I could manage to say. I felt like someone had torn open my intestines and stirred. I hadn't even thought of him dying. I could feel tears stinging the back of my eyes.

"Would you like to see him?" Robin asked. "You could come back with us, just for the night if you like?"

I desperately wanted to go with her and yet I shook my head fiercely.

"No. I can't. I've ..." but I couldn't say anything further. Robin placed a hand on my shoulder, but I shrugged it away and then I turned and moved. She called after me, but I couldn't respond.

I found myself running through the markets, chased by the startled and angry yells of a mutant whose apple cart I'd knocked over as I escaped.

I didn't go out again after that. I locked myself in Knife's house and grew. I applied my cream, and I thought on everything that had happened to me, and I wondered about Lowen and how he was faring. I wondered whether I should go back. I wondered why I couldn't. But mostly, I waited. And waited. Until, eventually, the time for my second harvest was upon me.

Majoris walked quickly, but I forced my weak legs to keep up. It was the middle of the day and it was hot under the bulky girdle that squeezed my folded skin against my body. But that wasn't going to slow me. I marched behind Majoris, determined. *This is the only way,* I repeated Knife's words to myself. The only way. And I almost believed it until the Compound gates came into view.

The feeling of dread that had been building in the pit of my stomach over the last weeks consumed me then, and without consciously willing anything to change, I found myself at a halt, standing in the middle of the road.

Majoris continued to stride ahead for a few paces before she sensed I was no longer following. She pulled up, and then turned to look at me, her expression confused and slightly annoyed.

"We're going to be late, Fennel," she said.

I swallowed, thinking back to my last visit to the Compound. Thinking to the work I'd done in the community. Thinking of Lowen.

"If there'd been another way for you, a way to survive that didn't hurt, that … that didn't steal so much from you, would you have taken it?"

Majoris stared at me, into me, like she was trying to determine my state of mind.

"This isn't really the time, Fennel. We need to get going."

"Please," I said.

She held my gaze a little longer, but then she glanced away and sighed.

"I had options, other diseases. But they all have costs. And rewards. I sold my skin, but now I'm clean. The same could happen for you if you do your time."

I swallowed again. I didn't believe her, not really.

"What if you could have lived clean from the beginning?"

A laugh escaped her, like something unpleasant she was spitting out.

"Like the residents, you mean? That's not for me."

"Because they wouldn't accept you?" I replied.

She snorted.

"Because even if they did, that's no way to live. They've locked themselves in a prison to keep away from people that they've imagined are beneath them. But we're all the same, really. I prefer to live my life freely, amongst real people."

"But how were you living freely when you sold your skin to them?"

"I'm free now. I'm clean."

"And what about me?" I whispered.

Majoris shrugged.

"You do the best with what you've got."

What did I have, I wondered? Leathered skin for selling, a brain for scheming, hands for sewing, legs to pull a plough. I shook my head.

"Come, we're late."

"No," I stated, and as I did, relief washed over me. "I can't. I'm done."

"Fennel, please. They're ready for us."

"No," I said again, more firmly. Majoris' eyes narrowed in response, and her lips formed a thin, angry line.

"You do this, my door is shut to you. There's no returning if you spurn me now."

"I know."

I stood at the foot of the dirt path looking up towards the ramshackle, mud brick building just shy of the creek. A few workers in white garments stopped to look at me, but they soon returned to their work as I began the trek up the hill.

Knife had tried to talk me out of my decision, but he hadn't succeeded. I knew he'd never understand, but I left him details of where I was going anyway, just in case.

Word of my arrival must have spread for, by the time I reached the top of the path, Robin was waiting for me.

I stopped before her, aware of my rough skin, the mounds of flesh held in place by my girdle. After our last meeting in Southwell, I didn't know what to say. Thankfully, she spoke first.

"I'm glad you came back, Fennel. And so is Lowen. He'd like to see you now if you'd like to see him?"

I nodded, grateful she'd made things easy for me.

I followed Robin into the hall and then through to the sleeping quarters. It was as I remembered, except one corner had been partitioned off with blankets hung from crude beams. It was to that corner that Robin guided me.

She gave me a gentle pat on the shoulder and then pulled the blankets aside.

The scent of rot hit me first and I stalled on the edge of the crude room. A tiny figure was huddled under a white blanket in the far corner, a wooden pail to the right, a jug of water on the left.

"Fennel, is that you?" Lowen croaked, and suddenly the figure moved, rolling onto his back. I took a couple of shallow breaths, then stepped inside and knelt down next to Lowen. Robin allowed the blanket to fall back into place, leaving the two of us alone.

He looked hideous. The top of the blanket was stained black from the tar leaking unbidden from his mouth and nose. His face was a mass of tumours. If he could still see through his yellow, weeping eyes, it couldn't be much. His tusk had grown larger and hair was spreading down his neck. God only knew what his limbs looked like underneath the blankets.

"It's me," I said. "And I'm so sorry. I should have come to see you earlier."

He shook his head.

"You have nothing to apologise for."

"I do. I've been so naive. I thought there was an easier way. But nothing's easy. Nothing."

"No. It's not. But some things are worth working for. A community. A home. Are you coming home now, Fennel?"

I cleared my throat.

"You'd have me back?"

"Of course," he whispered.

I didn't know why, but I burst into tears.

"How can you be so kind?" I blubbered. "How can you still want to help me after what I did, after what you saw of my true self?"

He just smiled again.

"We all make mistakes, Fennel."

"You don't. You were right," I said. "I met another resident. She was nothing like you. Cold, aloof. She looked at me like ... like I was nothing. Like I didn't matter. Like I was just something to use and buy and sell."

"Fennel, she was more like me than you know. At least, the boy I once was."

I sniffed loudly and looked at him, confused. But he didn't hold my gaze. Instead, he closed his eyes tight. I saw a tear escape and roll towards his nose.

"When we first met, you asked me why I left the Compound," Lowen said, his eyes still firmly shut. "I left my home and contracted this disease for penance, Fennel. It was what I had to do to make amends."

He took a deep breath, opened his eyes and looked at me. I could see his pain. His shame. His self-hate.

"When I was young," he began, "I used to tour Central with my friends. It's what the residents did. We would egg each other on, take advantage, lord it over the diseased. But that's no excuse for what we did. What I did." He took a deep breath. "She was about your age, Fennel. And we lied to her. And then we hurt her. We hurt her so badly and —"

I leaned forward and put my finger to his hot, black lips, quietening him.

"I don't need to know," I whispered. "Whatever it was, however horrible, you've changed. You've paid your dues."

More tears surfaced in his eyes and then ran down his cheeks.

"Nothing I have done can ever undo what I did. But I can keep trying. Will you let me keep trying, Fennel? Will you let me take your disease?"

He couldn't forgive himself, I saw. Either that or he wouldn't. But letting him take one last time, well that was something I could do. Something that I wanted to do, for him and me.

"Yes."

Lowen died three days later. The whole community was there to bury him.

Soon after, and I couldn't tell you why, Robin asked me to accompany her into town to help her recruit. Maybe she had good instincts, because it turned out I had a knack for it. While Robin had a kind heart, her spruiking was never as compelling or as passionate as Lowen's. Whereas I had something different to offer. I had the authenticity of an unbeliever. I was the first person ever to experience the community and then leave. And people wanted to know why I returned.

Sure, I still got the laughter and jeers, but a lot of people also listened to what I had to say — about my love of the Compound, my plan to get inside, my diseases, how I had tried the community, left, and then returned when I realised the true cost of participating in the society imposed upon us by the residents.

And each time I spoke, people came back with us.

Lowen started something decent out here. A new way for people to live as people. It's hard work. Really hard. And it's definitely not perfect. But nothing is, I realise now.

Great sacrifice is required, not least from Robin and the other takers who will eventually give up their lives so that we can live ours. But we have no shortage of new recruits. And the bigger we get, the stronger the community grows.

There are going to be struggles to come. The city has begun to take note of us. Just the other day, three cleans were beaten by an angry mob that accused them of taking their children and workers.

But I see that we need to press on. The community was possible because of Lowen's dream and his sacrifice. But it will only live if we live it, and grow if we grow it, by bringing it to those people who don't know this life is an option yet — people like I used to be.

About the story

I read an amazing short story called 'The Wombly' by K. L. Morris (*Shimmer Magazine*, Issue 32). Womblys are strange things that attach themselves to people, turning those people into soap, or metal, or glass, depending on the type of Wombly. A Wombly can be passed to someone else to bear and, once they are, they can't be passed back. The story dealt with a family sharing the burden of a soap Wombly, where a young girl was asked to ultimately bear the affliction for her family.

I thought the concept in 'The Wombly' was fascinating. It led me to imagining some of my own terrible diseases. The first disease I explored was the laid-to-waste disease. I began to pull together a story about a character with this disease — I even wrote a few introductory scenes — but, I ended up putting that story aside as it was becoming a bit too depressing and predictable. Which is when I began to wonder if bearing a disease was all bad. Maybe, diseases could have some useful side effects — useful enough to make money from at least.

So, 'This Side of the Wall' really began with that concept. I thought up a bunch of diseases that were both debilitating and useful, and I created a city around them. I already had a character with the laid-to-waste disease, so I threw him into the story, along with a few others to see how they'd react. And what I discovered was that some of these people were happy to accept a life of disease, while some aspired for more – to join the residents in the Compound, for example – and still others wanted to create a new and better world for themselves.

A question for the author

Q: Do you write things other than speculative fiction?

A: No, not really. Whenever I start developing a story thinking it might not be speculative, at some point my imagination runs away with me and the finished product ends up including something supernatural, or strange, or weird.

It's what I enjoy reading, and it's what I enjoy writing. I love great characters, and reading about interesting people. But I think characters react in even more fascinating ways when you throw them into a speculative world, or you have them face some fantastic or horrifying scenario.

About the author

Michael Gardner is a public servant and economist living in Canberra, Australia with his wife and two kids. He loves contemporary fantasy and horror – really anything strange or weird. And he has a very patient wife who puts up with his taste in TV shows and movies, and lets him spend more time writing then he probably should.

Memory is a Rumor

Yaroslav Barsukov

In the heat, even paper seemed to sweat. Dr. Startsev's fingers left wet stains on the pages of the open notebook, on a number: thirty. Thirty minutes to try and deter the people about to enter his office from doing the irreversible.

He always hoped for thirty; but when the front door in the lobby opened and steps drummed on the laminated floorboards, a resolute ostinato, he corrected himself: at most, twenty.

Then a male voice rang, the barking 'a's and the rolling 'r's, and Startsev was down to fifteen.

Through the blooming headache, he imagined Mr. Turkin answering the receptionist: "I'm here to replace my son."

Something rolled and rumbled in the street, and the noise made Startsev realize that his hand on the table had convulsed into a fist. *What the hell is wrong with you, old boy, calm down, calm down, they aren't even in the room yet.*

Nerves would only hurt the kid's chances.

Mr. Turkin wouldn't say 'replace', of course—people like him never shared Startsev's views on character grafting, people driving imported Bentleys, people sipping Bacardi in sunlit lounges at midday, life's marketers and lenders. The man's knowledge of the procedure likely stemmed from the ads in glossy magazines; Mr. Turkin would say 'enhance.'

The door into the office, opening, threw a shadow over the glass cases on the shelf: butterflies, brush strokes of wings melting in the summer heat. Startsev had started the collection in the third grade; he no longer knew why, but now, as the pieces of the July sun slipped back into the picture-like frames, something stirred in him, and a silly thought occurred:

maybe, if he saved the boy, he could remember.

"Good morning, Doctor."

"Good morning, Mr. Turkin, Mrs. Turkin. Kolya. Please, come in, take a sit."

They moved, figures assuming their places on a ghostly chessboard: the father, looking more like a hipster than an oligarch in his slim trousers, designer shorts, and sneakers, put on as though by accident; the mother, in a black-and-white polka-dot dress; and the son, a shorter figure trudging between them, clutching a mechanical dinosaur in his hands.

The boy. Kolya. Startsev's fingers spasmed again, and he forced himself to concentrate, try to piece together the parents' decision process: 'A bit too plump, a bit too passive for his age, stares at his toes all the time.' Over the phone, Mr. Turkin had summed his son up in one word: 'Slow.'

"I wonder if I've seen you before, Doctor." Mrs. Turkin lowered herself into a chair. "On TV, maybe?"

An acute feeling pricked Startsev, of being out of fashion, like an obsolete cell phone.

"Darling, please."

Mr. Turkin remained standing—and so did Kolya, after stealing a glance at his father.

"I'll repeat my question from yesterday: I'd like to know why we've been called here, after all the tests. My son has been through psychological and physical evaluations."

"It's not about tests," Startsev said and cringed inside at his own words. "This is an assessment of you as a family."

"Which our psychologist has already carried out," Mr. Turkin said. "How else could we've gotten a referral to this clinic?"

"We perform random checks to ensure the quality of practicing psychologists' work."

"So we've drawn the wrong ticket." Mr. Turkin nudged Kolya towards a chair and took the place next to him.

Startsev made an effort to smile. "I would look at this rather as an opportunity to get to know each other."

Mrs. Turkin stretched her hand behind Kolya's back to touch her husband's shoulder. She said, "It's fine, Doctor, we'll of course cooperate. And by the way, I'm sure now I've seen you on TV."

Mr. Turkin said, "On *Malakhov's Show,* probably. They like doctors. I take it then you'll be doing the operation?"

"No, I don't operate on patients anymore."

"Then? ..." A hand gesture, as though inviting Startsev to speak.

Then what the hell are you good for? Why are you intruding on my time?

Startsev said, "We're getting ahead of ourselves."

Kolya turned and looked back at the door; perhaps, on an unconscious level, searching for an escape.

A black leather document folder, snapping open. Startsev couldn't beg—a doctor begging just scared people; he had to follow the established dynamic, slide along the accepted routes, play the game. "This photograph. Could you tell me about the man, the donor? I may have seen the face somewhere, but I can't quite place him. Why have you chosen him for the character graft?"

The guy on the picture had a jaw which seemed wider than the rest of his head, a stretched smile turning his eyes into a pair of slits.

"Andrey Arshavin," Mr. Turkin said. "Midfielder in *Zenit,* the best footballer in the game right now."

"Does that mean you're interested in soccer, Kolya?"

The boy pressed the dinosaur against his chest. "Doctor, I—"

"He isn't," Mr. Turkin said.

"Then why this Arshavin fellow?"

Mrs. Turkin produced a neat little smile. "Our psychologist recommended him, and we both like the way Andrey plays."

"Dr. Petrov did a comprehensive analysis," her husband said. "Full mapping of Kolya's brain, plus nine or ten surveys. I mean, put together, how long have you spent in his office, Tatyana?— yeah, at least a day. He said Andrey Arshavin is the perfect donor for the character traits Kolya needs."

The yellow card in the document folder said, 'Resilience, competitiveness, will for success.' A fly, half-comatose from the heat, crawled onto Startsev's hand and stopped between the two bulges of veins. Sweat, palpable against the onset of a headache, burned a line on the back of his neck.

Concentrate, Startsev thought.

He said, "Kolya's eight years old."

The boy drew in a breath. "Eight and a half."

"Please do not interrupt the doctor," Mr. Turkin said.

"He didn't interrupt me at all—and thank you for correcting me, Kolya. At this age, how do you know he's not resilient enough?"

"He's afraid of math tests."

"I probably was too when I was eight."

Mr. Turkin leaned forward. "He's slow, he's not measuring up to his classmates. He has a 'Satisfactory' in math. A 'Satisfactory.'"

Startsev slapped his palm on the desk; he did it to shake off the fly, but the crack of flesh against wood broke some dam inside him. "Then maybe Kolya's the next Mendeleev. Mendeleev had mediocre marks at school. You yourself, Mr. Turkin, did you ever get anything above 'Satisfactory' in math?"

The man leaned forward in his chair. "Doctor, are you *absolutely* sure your guidelines include insulting your customers?"

Back off, rethink. No lashing out, not with these people, old boy. "Please forget what I've said." Startsev fanned his fingers and patted the table. "Must be the heat. The air conditioner's been dead for days."

"To answer your question, Doctor, we *are* certain he's lagging behind," Mr. Turkin said, "because our psychologist has told us that if we don't act now, Kolya would never reach his full potential."

"The potential—I'm sorry, Mr. Turkin, his potential, by definition, is right here in front of you."

Husband and wife stared at him. Kolya turned to look at the door again; no, not the door, Startsev realized: the boy studied the shelf, aquamarine wings in glass cases.

"Do you like my butterflies?"

Kolya jerked his head back around and straightened. He didn't appear frightened, only a little anxious: he must've sensed the tension in the room, but eight years was too gentle an age to comprehend the full gravity of the conversation. His fingers let go of the dinosaur and reached for his mother's hand.

"Go on, answer the question," Mr. Turkin said.

"I love bugs, Doctor. Insects, I mean. They're so different from us, like aliens..."

Something squeezed inside Startsev. *All the little worlds, we step on. That's what we're good at, stepping on precious little worlds, trampling them underfoot.*

You cannot, you cannot beg for him.

Mr. Turkin shrugged. "Spends weekends in the garden—"

Mrs. Turkin said, "We have a big garden."

"—taking pictures of beetles and such, can you imagine that? He takes photos and then, for a whole hour, arranges them on his table."

Without thinking, Startsev said, "I rearrange my butterflies too, every morning."

He immediately regretted the words, a part of himself he hadn't meant to share.

"Why do you rearrange them, Doctor?" the boy said.

"I... Doesn't matter." As though in a dream, Startsev glanced at the butterflies, wishing he could see them through the boy's eyes. Then he caught himself and forced his thoughts onto the more practical rails. "Mr. Turkin, Kolya may become an entomologist or a botanist. You should be proud; most kids of his age have no hobby at all."

The boy batted his eyelashes, and Startsev thought, *They don't praise him even a bit.*

Mr. Turkin sniffed. "Not much of a hobby. I'm not raising him to end up a loser. Ever heard of a millionaire botanist, Doctor? Money and success are in the financial sector."

Mrs. Turkin said in an apologizing tone, "We want him to be a winner."

Startsev rested his head on his fingers —*think, think*—trying to come up with next move the way a chess player would. He wished for the sun to stop, he wished it were evening already. Watercolor wings now seemed like eyes, gazing at him accusingly from the shelf.

"The operation, Kolya," he said, "do you have any idea what it entails?"

The boy hesitated and glanced at his father. "I want to become tough."

Startsev turned to Mr. Turkin. "Could we have a word alone?"

"If we must. Son, sit outside."

Behind the glass panel by the door, Kolya's silhouette slouched into a chair in the lobby. Dangling legs, just long enough for the toes to touch the floor. Hands, fumbling with the leg of the mechanical dinosaur.

Mr. Turkin said, "What kind of family assessment is this? I don't understand what you're trying to achieve, Doctor, but

I'm this close to leaving—and then I'm going to have a talk with whoever runs this establishment."

"I'd like to describe the procedure to you," Startsev said. "Because some think we do it with magnets and lasers. What really happens is, we sedate the patient, and then we peel away the skin." He made a gesture as though taking off a hat. "Saw through the bone. Then the surgeon takes the scalpel and makes an incision, cuts into the lump of meat. At this point, the brain is just meat, and you need to cut it for the machines to go in and reshape the neural pathways. The doctor who operates the machines flashes a light into the opening every now and again to make sure nothing got jammed, and if you peek in at that instant, you see metal working inside the brain. Inside the *person.* And in my experience, the *person* who leaves the operation room is never the same one that has entered it. Whatever you may think, it's not an enhancement."

They waited.

"Do you realize how the grafting of character traits came to be?" Startsev said. "It branched off from a different procedure; 'personality transplant' as we called it."

Still, they waited.

"It was conceived as a remedy for schizophrenia."

"I know," said the father. "We researched online before coming here. Character grafts are trivial in comparison. Like, you've rules for it, the graft must not constitute more than ten percent..." He waved his hand.

"Mr. Turkin, as somebody once told me, there's no scientific definition of an individual. No definition of you or me. How much can you replace before the old 'you' ceases to exist? Twenty percent? Forty? Forty-five? If you take your son on a fishing trip, it's the most amazing thing in the world to him, and then a year later he can't even remember the occasion—is he still the same person?"

"We don't do fishing trips," Mr. Turkin said. "Fishing trips are a waste of time."

"Mrs. Turkin," Startsev said, "his dinosaur—the toy—things he loves right now, he may not love them afterwards."

He glimpsed a flash of fear in her eyes, and panic pricked him. How much time did he have left? He'd been wrong, he'd been wrong since the first moment, he should've concentrated on the mother, the mother was the key. Perhaps...

She said, "But he will still love *me?*"

Startsev opened and closed his mouth. Then he dropped his gaze to the documents as though he hoped to find there a cue which would allow him to say 'no.' "Love for one's mother is a deep-going instinct," he said quietly. "Kolya will keep loving you, yes. And yet I'd like you to consider carefully what you're doing. Please. Your son, the one that just exited the room, will die."

She rose her hand to her lips in a quick gesture, then said, "But I thought the mortality rates were zero."

Startsev studied Mr. and Mrs. Turkin: two human beings separated from him by an invisible, impenetrable wall. A decade ago, when that moment had come during his first prep talk, a part of him, inside, screamed, and scratched, and fumed, and fought for the control of the motor neurons—but years dull one's edge. Repetition upon repetition, they wash away everything but the underlying fatigue. He wished it were evening and he could curl in the corner of his office and cease listening, seeing, thinking.

He leaned back in his chair and took out a pen.

That's it, old boy. Let it go.

"This week is booked. I can put you down for next Tuesday."

They signed the papers.

At the door, Mr. Turkin paused, holding his hand on the knob. "This was no family assessment, was it, Doctor?"

"Goodbye, Mr. Turkin."

"I know where Tatyana saw you. I recognize you now. You're one of the graft's fathers. One of the original team? What are you trying to do, sabotage your own work?"

"Goodbye to both of you."

After the door slammed shut, Startsev leaned back in his chair and pressed his fingers against his forehead. *You're right, Mr. Turkin.* Sabotage was a strong word, though; his old colleagues had all but tied his hands—and they would've gladly removed him, too, hadn't he held a significant share of the stock.

What remained were these prep conversations: hardly sabotage, only a tiny chance of dissuading people from making the biggest mistake of their lives.

A handful of successes over a decade of failures—but still, he kept trying: his own private little war against human nature.

Through the glass, he saw the parents talking to Kolya; following an impulse,

Startsev stood, picked up a butterfly from the shelf, and went into the lobby.

Behind the window, the far end of the street squirmed in the heat haze. Startsev watched the family exit the hospital; Kolya trudged between his parents, glass case under his arm. He took his mother's hand.

Startsev turned and regarded the insects on the shelf. One was missing now, but he surmised, with weariness, that it would return to its place on Tuesday.

Once, the butterflies had been important to him, but he no longer knew why, and no rearrangement of cases would help that. He didn't remember his own operation; he recalled the rationale— he was a remnant of an age when scientists believed the first test subjects should be themselves—but not the feeling. What had *that man* felt, lying down on the operating table and breathing in the first curls of anesthetic gas?

Memory is an internal rumor, he thought. Perhaps the old Startsev had never existed; perhaps it had always been him, in the white lab coat, in this office, staring at a collection of butterflies that belonged to somebody else.

A question for the author

Q: Have you ever wondered whether ideas are thought waves directed at you by an AI supercomputer located in the distant future?

A: I have, actually. I don't know where ideas come from or why it's sometimes so easy to forget them; it's as though someone would hand you a Post-it note and, in case you don't display an immediate interest, pass it on.

Why does the supercomputer have to reside in the future though? I'm a big proponent of digital physics, Universe as an output of a computer program and all, and I strongly suspect that we and everything around us is a simulation. As soon as I say it, people immediately think *Matrix*; but what if there's nothing else *but* the simulation? What if there's no real us, or beings like us, outside the program's boundaries?

The thought, to me, is too sad not to be true.

About the author

Yaroslav Barsukov is a software engineer from Moscow, currently living in Vienna, Austria. After leaving his ball and chain at the workplace, he goes on to write stories that deal with things he himself, thankfully, doesn't have to deal with.

www.facebook.com/tem.sweenoff, @YBarsukov

Copyright

Metaphorosis Publishing

Metaphorosis offers beautifully written science fiction and fantasy. Our projects include:

Metaphorosis Magazine

Metaphorosis, a weekly magazine of SFF short stories, including stories from all the authors in this anthology. Find out more at magazine.metaphorosis.com, and sign up to be notified of new stories.

Metaphorosis Books

Recent books from Metaphorosis can be found at <u>books.metaphorosis.com</u>, and include:

Metaphorosis 2017   **Metaphorosis 2016**

All the stories from *Metaphorosis* magazine's second year.

Almost all the stories from *Metaphorosis* magazine's first year.

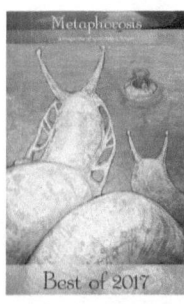

**Metaphorosis:
Best of 2017**

The best science
fiction and fantasy
stories from
Metaphorosis' 2nd
year.

**Metaphorosis:
Best of 2016**

The best science
fiction and fantasy
stories from
Metaphorosis' 1st
year.

Reading 5X5

Five stories, five times

Twenty-five SFF authors, five base stories, five versions of each – see how different writers take on the same material.

Reading 5X5

Writers' Edition

All the stories from the regular, readers' edition, plus two extra stories, the story seed, and authors' notes.

Best Vegan SFF of 2017

The best vegan science fiction and fantasy stories of 2017!

Best Vegan SFF of 2016

The best vegan science fiction and fantasy stories of 2016!

Susurrus

A darkly romantic story of magic, love, and suffering.

www.ingramcontent.com/pod-product-compliance
Lightning Source LLC
Chambersburg PA
CBHW020527120726
47904CB00003B/993